What people are saying about

Mistfall in the Grove of Dreams

A truly magical story that captured my imagination from beginning to end! This gripping modern take on the path to inner wisdom is enchanting, with a serious twist in the tale that will leave you wanting more! I couldn't put it down until finished.
Nina Ashby, author of *Develop Your ESP* and *Simply Colour Therapy*

Mistfall in the Grove of Dreams

Mistfall in the Grove of Dreams

Paul R. Harrison

Winchester, UK
Washington, USA

First published by Roundfire Books, 2019
Roundfire Books is an imprint of John Hunt Publishing Ltd., No. 3 East St., Alresford,
Hampshire SO24 9EE, UK
office1@jhpbooks.net
www.johnhuntpublishing.com
www.roundfire-books.com

For distributor details and how to order please visit the 'Ordering' section on our website.

Text copyright: Paul R. Harrison 2018

ISBN: 978 1 78904 008 1
978 1 78904 009 8 (ebook)
Library of Congress Control Number: 2017964340

A CIP catalogue record for this book is available from the British Library.

Design: Stuart Davies

Printed and bound by CPI Group (UK) Ltd, Croydon, CR0 4YY, UK

We operate a distinctive and ethical publishing philosophy in
all areas of our business, from our global network of authors to
production and worldwide distribution.

Acknowledgments

Thanks are due to the people who provided background to this story over many years. In particular, I would like to thank Douglas Ashby, Nina Ashby, Catherine Kavanagh, Arlene Rock, Gail Dawkins, Christine Shirley, Joanna Lowther and past and present members of the Foundations for Holistic Consciousness. In addition, major influences have included Theo Gimbel, Elaine Walker, Michael Armstrong and Mike Daly, without whom none of it would have been possible. Thank you, everyone.

PART I

Chapter 1

I wake up in pain, as always. The sun is only just up, but light filters between the sticks. At the other end of the room, the goat snorts. My mother sleeps on; she always awakes a little after me. There is no food, but the thought of a crust later pushes me from my wooden bed.

I leave and follow the way downhill. I use the three stones to step across the stream, pausing on the middle one so I can kneel down and drink from the cool flow. Some say that Peter the old smith died because he drank water too far down, and did not use the village well. That sounds wrong. I do not understand how drinking water can end your life.

I walk down the hill, past the wall which runs around the big field, with the gap in it big enough for a person, but too small for a beast. The sheep are waking. As is my habit, I stand in the gap for a moment, looking across the field to the far wall, and beyond it, the forest, treetops brightened by the early sun, but deep and dark within. The gap over there leads to the path through the forest, which leads to Dol Ham, the next village. Some folk go there once a week for the market. I have never left my home. Michael says that there are wolves in the forest, but he has had a summer less than me, so I do not think he really knows. I asked my mother one evening. She fell asleep before she could answer. I am sure it must be wonderful to go through the forest to another place and meet people you do not know. Michael says that there are big villages, with more people than anyone can count. I cannot believe it and, anyway, how would he know? It does not sound right to me; you could not feed so many people.

In the village, I stop at the well, pull up the bucket and use the deep spoon to take another mouthful. Mary passes me. She is making her way to the dairy. She smiles and her face lights up. I smile back, but cannot hold a look at her face, as I am too shy. She will have butter later today, but not cheese, never on a Saturn day.

I pass the round church. It will be full tomorrow, as usual. Outside is the old cross, with the circle around it. Many still pray there, after the Sun day worship, just to be safe. Others still talk of Pan and the Green Man and the gods of the forest, but they say that doing so is dangerous. I do not see how believing something can be dangerous. But I do not understand grown people yet.

Just past the church, in a small field, there stands my favourite thing in the world: the small ring of stones, ten paces across. When I am going home, I like to stop there and sit in the middle, or on the biggest stone. I remember when I could only sit on the smallest stone. Nobody knows why it is there, but I sit there and I like it. That is all I know about the stones: I like them. Somebody must know why they were put there, but nobody is saying.

As I reach the far side of the village, where the stream widens and completes its circuit around the back of the homes, I can already hear the creak of the wheel, and think I can spot John, the miller, at the far side of it, scraping the green stuff off. I scurry past the millpond—no ducks today—and the mill dam, renewed this spring by the men. John greets me. 'Be here before the sun hits the church, lad,' he told me on my first day as his apprentice, some four years ago. Sometimes, I am late and he takes a stick to me, but he is fair and a good man.

John has taught me all about the mill. How the water turns the wheel, which turns the top stone. 'Stand clear, lad! Topstone moving!' is his cry every morning as he sets it in motion. He has taught me about how the stone has moods. Sometimes it sulks, and has tears. Sometimes it is happy and bone dry. The moods tell you how long to leave it grinding. When I said the day was cold once, he taught me of the danger of making fire in a mill. Of course, the mill could burn. I knew that. But the dust can make

3

a terrible flash, with noise and power. I did not know that. He is clever. That is John the miller's cleverness. Some days, I think I want to be the miller and tend the stone, to make the flour, to give to the baker to make bread and to give to Mary to make apple pies so she can give me a slice with cream she has churned. John is happy; milling must make you happy.

There are a lot of things I am unable to do yet. I can pull the grain bags up to the top using the pulley, but I cannot lift the bags of flour. John does that. 'One day you'll have big arms, lad,' he tells me. I want arms like John's one day.

He greets me with a red-cheeked smile and he grabs a crust — today there is butter! — and thrusts it into my hand. I tear at it, greedily, and give him a big smile. It is good bread, made from good flour by a good man. 'You have to love your work,' he tells me, often. 'Then your love goes into it and what you make is good.' It is sound advice. I like the mill and I like John, but I am not sure if I would love being a miller. Of course, we do not choose our lot in life, but whatever lot life gives us, we have to make the most of it. I think it is important to do your best.

The work is hard, but John the miller is kind. I cannot carry heavy things, but the amount of lifting that I can do makes the pain in my back get worse. But that is life. We have to lift things and suffer. One day, I will go to our Lord and rest.

Chapter 2

I wake up in pain. Today, something is different. The sun is not up. Why am I awake? The goat is asleep. My mother is asleep. But I am awake.

I listen. There is no sound. I am lying on my side with a bag of feathers between my knees to ease my back. I roll over onto my back and see him.

A few paces from the bottom of my bed, there is a tall man, shrouded in darkness. He just stands there, looking down at me. I sit up, afraid. Men in your home, or even just in the village, can be dangerous. A stranger passed through the village last year and punched David full in the face. There was no reason for it. David is good and friendly. He has the same number of summers as me. Now he walks with his head on one side and cannot talk well and he has spit dripping from his mouth. He was a friend.

The stranger does not move, just stands and stares. He is simply dressed. It is night, but I think I can see a white robe, reaching to the floor, held at the waist by a cord. There are shoes on his feet, but they are more like leather straps than shoes. He stands there, unmoving. Should I speak? He might be highborn and be angry at me speaking out of turn, so I look back at him, as humbly as I can. Something is not right, apart from him being there. Something is strange...

I thought it was a trick of the light, but there is almost no light, just a silver softening of the darkness caused by the waxing gibbous in the clear night sky. Then why does he glow? A gentle, shifting golden light dances around his body. I chance a word. 'Welcome, sir,' I say softly, both to be respectful and not to wake my mother. He stares and I feel sleepy. I blink, or did I sleep? When I open my eyes, he is gone.

Should I wake my mother? She would not thank me for robbing her of sleep. She needs it so much. As do I, but this is a strange thing to happen and it takes me some time to sleep.

I wake with the sun. My back hurts. The goat snorts at the other end. My mother sleeps on.

The Sabbath. While I wait for my mother to awake, I go into the village. Down the hill, past the wall round the big field. I look as deeply as I can into the dark wood. Birds call. The sheep in the wood field graze quietly, the sun climbs, the smell of green plants and wildflowers reaches me. All is silence, apart from the stream, tinkling over small pebbles, the low sun flashing off the water.

Past the round church, the circle cross and the holy well and into the stone circle. This is my favourite time of the week, summer or winter. Alone, silent, surrounded by the guardian stones. After a few minutes sitting there, the pain in my back diminishes. The good feeling will last until mid Moon day morn, when the toil at the mill will bring it back.

The sun is coming up and it is warm. Why, then, is there mist by the stones? It is not like a normal mist, lying just above the grass and making me wet as I sit. It is all around the stones, right to the tops. I cast my gaze across the circle. It is on every stone. It glows oddly, reminding me of the man at the foot of my bed, but not really moving in the way it did around him. The mist round one stone joins the mist of its neighbour, all along the circle. It comes together inside the ring and, just in front of Long Hec, the biggest stone, it gathers and thickens. I go and sit in that spot. I feel light, as if I could fly. I hear—but do not hear—a strange word: 'Ulph', as if it is whispered on the wind, except there is no wind and it is in my head. I do not know much, but I know it is not a word I have ever heard. I did not see any augers on my walk here, but it is a day for strange things, nonetheless.

I pass the dairy on the way back. Mary is up and beckons me over. She gives me milk to take home. I thank her and she gifts me that smile.

Passing the dry wall, I slip into the forest field and gather plants.

Back at home, my mother is awake. I grab the flint and start a fire. I heat water and chop plants to put in it. There is still a little honey left, but not enough for two, so I put it in my mother's cup because she is very fond of the sweet flavour. I pour some milk. When she has supped and is fully awake, I venture a question.

'Mother, there was a man in here early this morning. Before sun. Do you know who it might be?'

'A man? Someone from the village?'

'No, Mother. A stranger. He had on a white robe which went down to his feet, and he wore shoes of leather strips. And there was something strange.'

'More strange than that?' she asks.

'He had a strange light about him.'

She stares at the fire, as if she is thinking, as if she is remembering something.

'And Mother, what is Ulph?'

She flashes me a look. I am frightened for a moment.

'Where did you hear that, boy? Speak now!'

I have never seen my mother like this. She is often frightened, as we all are, but her look is mixed with another feeling. I cannot name it, but it is like wonder, or curiosity, or just fear of something else.

'I sat in the stones and I thought I heard it on the wind. Sorry, Mother, did I do a bad thing?'

She gazes at me, wide-eyed. Then her look softens and she gives me her own, wonderful smile.

'My son,' she says, pulling me towards her. 'Don't be afraid.'

After the church, all the villagers head to their homes. My mother pulls me to the side of them as they come out of the round church.

'Straight home now. I need to speak to Master Thomas.' She heads off in the opposite direction to home.

This truly is a day for strange things. Master Thomas, the

head of the village, has the largest home of all of us. It is on the opposite hill. I have never spoken to him, although he has spoken to me on holy day gatherings in the well square, just to say good day. He is the bravest and the wisest. If strangers come, they must all see Master Thomas. If someone wants to build, Master Thomas will organise the villagers to help. But my mother never visits him, never speaks to him. She is too lowly. I know he will be kind to her, for she is of the village, but I really want to know why she wishes to speak to him now. I want to understand.

What are these happenings today? Is it just me who is seeing them, or are others experiencing the strangeness?

The wonders do not stop. I am feeding the goat outside when they arrive.

My mother is there with Master Thomas. He stands in front of me and looks me up and down.

Then he speaks.

'Good day, lad.'

I look up at him. I am very frightened and cannot speak. My mother slaps me on my arm.

'What say you to Master Thomas, boy?' she says.

'Good day to you, M-master,' I stammer. The voice that comes out of me is tiny.

'Good day, lad. A strange day for you, I hear.'

'Yes, Master.' I dare not say more. How much does he know? Does he think me mad? Will he send me from the village, or put me to work cleaning pots, or sit me in the well square while people throw cabbages at me? Am I to be the idiot? I tremble.

'Fear not, lad. I have seen this before. Or something like it. You may be a wyrd one.'

I look at him wide-eyed. The head of the village is talking to me and I do not know his words. I am so frightened.

'Master?'

He does not answer my unspoken question.

'I have a special task for you tomorrow.'

'Thank you, Master.' This is it, I think. "Cabbage boy," they will call me. Everyone will laugh, even strangers.

'You are to go into the forest and spend the day in the dell. When you get back, you're to tell me all. You understand, lad?'

'Yes, Master.' I pause, then dare to say, 'But...' I stop.

'What is it, lad?'

'Please you, Master, I do not know the forest, or the dell.'

My mother speaks.

'He has never been into the woods, Master Thomas, not to Dol, nor anywhere.'

'I see. Then I will tell you.'

'Thank you, Master.'

He does so.

I am to go through the gap in the wall, across the field, through the gap in the far wall and take the way into the forest. After walking for as long as it takes to walk to John's mill and back, the way splits. The main path goes on to Dol. The way to the right, the narrow way, goes down and bends back towards the village. At the bottom is a clearing. I am to sit there all day. As the sun hits the treetops, I am to return home.

Chapter 3

I wake up with the sun. I notice that my back does not hurt. My mother is up, as she often is the day after the Sabbath. She is putting bread and cheese in a cloth, which she ties and hands to me. She also gives me a skin of water. She kisses me and I set off down the hill.

I stop on the middle of the stream stones and kneel for a drink. I think I am frightened, but I cannot be sure. The day is fair and warm already. Birds sing overhead and a gentle breeze comes up the hill. Fresh water drips off my chin. I wipe it away and see my hand is dark with dirt. I throw water over my face. I also wash my hands. It feels good. I have not been in the millpond this year, so I am probably dirty everywhere, but at least now my hands and face are clean.

I go down the hill. As I reach the gap in the wall I stop. I look at the sheep, slowly grazing and noisily bleating. I wonder if they know. Do they know the lord's men will take their wool and, later, their lives so that the lord can eat mutton? If they do not, why not? If they do, why not run away? I banish the thought and slip through the gap. The grass is wet with dew. Soon, my feet are cold and wet, but now they too are clean.

As I reach the gap in the far wall, I realise that when I take one more step, I will be farther from home than I have ever been. I have stood by this gap before, gazing into the dark of the forest, but I have always been frightened by the thought of wolves and other beasts, so I never stayed long. Now, I have to enter the forest.

Suddenly, I think of John the miller. He would be expecting me. It will be bad when I see him tomorrow. Unless my mother, or Master Thomas, thought to tell him. Surely they would. If not, he will be angry. But I cannot think of that today. I must do as I am bid. I take a deep breath and enter the forest.

After a few paces, the way climbs slightly. It is dim and I cannot see the sun. Here, I am between places. Not in my village, nor in the next village, nor yet in the clearing. I am moving between one place and another. A part of me wants to go back, to be hoisting bags of grain for John, but another part of me wants to know what is past the next tree.

Moss grows on stones and the tree sides, so I can find my way home. And, anyway, the path is clear and well-trodden by so many people before me. I trust in the knowledge that nobody I have heard of has been eaten by wolves, or got lost. Still, it is a little frightening. It is so quiet. The breeze has dropped and, for the most part, the only sound is of my feet as they crunch dry leaves and crack dry twigs. I stop for a moment and listen. There are sounds, although I have not noticed them until now. Birds tweet and flutter away from the high branches and unknown small beasts crackle through the undergrowth. There are smells, too. There are not many wildflowers, and yet a scent reaches my nose. I do not know it, so I think of it as the smell of the forest. The scent is a mixture of wood and damp and wild plants. I spot a few mushrooms. Most are good, but there are bad ones too. I do not know which is which, yet.

I think I have walked as if to the mill and back, so I look for the path. At first, I cannot see it but, as the path takes a bend, just past a tree, I see the path separate. The main way continues. Heading to the right is a narrower, less travelled path, mostly overgrown by grass and bracken.

This is it. I look back, but the village is gone. I look ahead up the main way, but it winds past tall trees and there is nothing but forest to see. I take a deep breath and step onto the narrower way.

Undergrowth tickles and scrapes against my legs. I am worried about beasts laying low, ready to pounce. The path curves round to the right and my spirits rise, as I start to think I am approaching the village and home. Then, I see it. Not the village, but a circular area of forest, treeless and low.

The path I am on widens and ends as I go down into the clearing. To walk across it would be like walking from home to the stream, so it is not large. There is flat grass, which looks soft and inviting after my walk, a small pond and some overhanging trees. And there is the sun! Still climbing, only just visible above the treetops. I rejoice inside, as I did not realise how much I had missed it in the forest.

At the far side of the clearing, there is a stone. It is round and flat. If a man lay down on it, he would just match its length.

Now that I am here, I am not sure what to do. I sit on the grass. It is dry and very comfortable. I dip my feet in the cool, flat pool. Ripples spread out and I watch them. All is silent. Even the forest beasts seem to sleep here. And the air is different. I cannot say how exactly. It seems to be calm and somehow deep, like the pool.

I take my feet out of the water and lie on the grass, gazing at the treetops and the clear blue sky. I like blues and greens best, I think, although I also like the flowers that grow at the foot of John's hill. In summer, they appear in bright blues, sun colour and light red. But I always love the sky and the grass best.

After a moment—I am not sure if I have dozed or not—I sit up. Something is strange. My senses are sharpened. I am not frightened. I am not certain it would be possible to be frightened in this place. But something is different. The sun is overhead now, so perhaps I did sleep a little.

I listen. I look. Nothing.

I look across the clearing. There is something about the stone. I want to go and sit on it, but something holds me back. I stare at it. Then something draws my attention. In the forest. Not the way I came, but the other side of the clearing. I feel as if there is something there. Or someone. Watching. I look deep into the branches. I see branches and nothing else.

I turn back to look at the stone. I get up and walk round the pond and stand in front of it. Something feels strange. I want to climb on it, to sit or lie down, but I cannot. Something stops me, as if gentle, invisible hands are on my shoulders. I cannot move forward. After a while, I give up and go back to the grass and sit.

It takes me a moment to realise that the sun has moved across the sky and is almost touching the far trees. How did this happen? A short time ago it was midday. I ponder this loss of time, as I take out my mother's cheese and bread. I realise I am hungry and wolf it down.

This makes me think of wolves. Darkness approaches and I remember the instructions of Master Thomas.

I run up the small way, rejoin the main one and run back to the village. I slip through the gap, cross the field, through the other gap and head up the hill to home.

My mother is waiting. It is still light, but the sun is falling fast. She says I am to see Master Thomas at once.

The fear returns. 'Now, Mother?'

'Aye. Off you go.'

It is almost dark. I have never been outside our home after dark.

As I approach Master Thomas's house, I tremble again. He is the head of the village and must be obeyed. Will he think me mad if I tell all? Will he know if I hold things back? I realise I must be truthful and hope for the best.

He welcomes me.

'Come in, lad. Now, tell me everything that happened today.'

I decide it is best to tell all as quickly as possible, and I do so, holding nothing back. The path, the clearing, the silence, the stone, the thing I felt was watching from the forest. And how time seemed strange.

To my surprise, he makes no comment. He listens and nods.

When I have finished, he says, 'Off to home with you, lad. Tell nobody what happened. We will talk tomorrow.'

I leave and head down the hill towards the village. As I start the climb towards home, I glance back and, in the last of the light, I see Master Thomas heading across the big field into the forest. He is brave to do this at night and I wonder where he is heading.

My mother says I should not worry. Master Thomas has my future in hand. She holds me for a moment. She does not usually do that.

That night, I dream I am floating in the air above the stone.

Chapter 4

The sun is already up when I wake. I am late. The goat has gone outside. I think of wolves, but then notice that my mother is not there. I am very late. John the miller will be angry. I jump up and go outside. I see the goat, but my mother is not here. This is strange.

I am exhausted, as if I have been travelling all night. That is also strange, because I did no work yesterday.

I go to the stream and take some water. Farther down the hill, I see Mary. She waves and beckons me. When I reach her, I tell her I am late and have to run up to the mill, but she stops me. She tells me, 'Your mother told me that, if I saw you pass, I was to stop you. You are to stay at home and wait for Master Thomas.' Once again, I think of people throwing cabbages. I shake a little. Mary notices and takes me inside.

In the dairy, she has bread and cheese, and gives me some. I thank her and bless her. I am nervous around Mary. I want to tell her all, as I am sure she would understand, but I remember Master Thomas. I do not want to make him angry. But I tell her that things have been strange. She smiles a little. I am sure she understands. Or is it that she knows something more than me, and there is a little sadness in that smile? Does she think me mad? A fool? Is she thinking about cabbages?

I finish breaking my fast. Mary says I should go.

Back at home, I talk to the goat. Then I go round the back to our tiny garden and water the vegetables. The rabbits have kept away since I built the low fence. The vegetables are growing well. There will be good pottage soon. The river has gudgeon and our lord lets us hunt squirrel, but I prefer my mother's pottage.

I tend the soil until my mother arrives. Another strange thing. She should be working. Master Thomas is with her.

'Now then, lad. Sit you down,' he says.

I sit on the ground. Master Thomas sits on the large rock outside our home. My mother stands next to him. She seems tired and afraid, but then she always does.

'Today, you are to go back to the dell. Someone will see you there. You will be staying a long time, so say goodbye to your mother.'

I go to her. She is still tired and afraid, but there is something else. I do not know the name, but it is a feel you have when someone you like or love does a fine thing. It is a good feel. She has a warm smile as she looks at me. She signals me to wait, goes inside and fetches a bundle. There is bread and cheese, she says.

'Always remember you are your parent's son. Hurry now. Time does not wait.'

She holds me for a moment and kisses my cheek. These are indeed strange days.

Master Thomas stands and places his hands on my shoulders.

'Learn fast and well, lad. We will see you again. Off with you, now.'

He gives me a gentle push towards the big field, the gap into the forest, and the path to the clearing.

As I walk, I wonder what I am to learn. I thought I was to be a miller.

As I cross the field, I notice that my tunic has more holes, threads hang off it everywhere, and it is now halfway up my upper leg. I do not have so much dirt on my legs and feet because it is summer. My arms and legs are very brown, so I suppose my face is brown too. All the sheep stop eating and look at me as I cross.

I remember the smell of the forest from yesterday. I like it. It is the earth and moss and plants and mushrooms.

Things are dry. The villagers are fearful of fire in the summer, so Master Thomas ordered a plan if there is fire. Some people are to carry earth, some water and some beating sticks. Master Thomas is good and wise and looks after his people in the village.

I reach the split in the path and head down to the clearing.

It is the same as yesterday and there is the same feel of calm and depth in the air. I see the pool and the rock. I see the trees. I see...what's this?

There is a house!

That is not possible. There was no house yesterday. Even Will the strong cannot build a house overnight. It is off to the side where I thought someone was watching. It is largely overgrown by the forest, but there is a clear space in front, a short path to the clearing. The door of the small house opens slowly. Someone steps out, but I cannot see them clearly. They stand for a while, then slowly move towards me.

It is an old woman. Maybe five tens of summers. I am not sure I have met anyone so old. My mother has two tens and eight, she thinks. I am ashamed to say that my mouth hangs open a little, not just at her age, but at why I did not see the house yesterday.

'I'm six tens and three, boy, if that's what you're thinking! And you did not see the house because I did not want you to see the house.'

I do not know what to say. How did she know? I stammer, like a village idiot.

'I beg your forgiveness, Lady, I did not mean to stare.'

She smiles and a tiny chuckle comes out.

'I am not a lady. A madwoman, some say, but not a lady.' Her chuckle escapes and the clearing suddenly seems a happy place. I smile. 'People call me Mother, so you might as well do the same.'

'Yes...' It feels awkward, as I think of my own mother. 'Mother.'

She stands in front of me. She looks into my eyes, then up and down the length of my short body, then she looks above my head for a time, then into the air to the right and left sides of my head. She smiles. It is a warm smile and I smile back. I hope she is pleased. I suddenly want to please her.

'I thought so. Right. In we go. We've got a lot to talk about.'

The house is full of good things. Plants sit in pots on shelves. I recognise some of them, but not others. The wooden floor is covered with a large cloth. There is a small table and two stools. In the corner, there is a roll of woollen cloth, which I suppose to be a bed. Another woollen sheet lies folded on a shelf above the bed. In the corner, there is a tall metal box with a hole in the front and a pipe on one side. The pipe goes through the roof. Inside the metal box there is a fire. A fire! Inside a house! Wood crackles. On top, there is a pan with something inside, bubbling.

'Sit you down.' Her voice is high and cracked. It sounds as if she is laughing when she speaks. Perhaps she is. She certainly seems to find me funny. I am a peasant boy in rags, so I am used to that from my betters. I sit on one of the stools.

Mother places two wooden bowls and two wooden spoons on the table. I admire the workmanship. Peter the woodsman makes all the bowls for the village, but they are not this fine.

She brings the pot to the table and uses a larger wooden spoon to lift the contents into my bowl.

'I usually eat vegetables. Same as you, I expect. Not because I have to, but because they taste better than meat. But today there is rabbit stew.'

I jump from the table and look around. I am in deep fear.

'But...' I say, trying to find the words for something so terrifying. 'But my mother says I must never kill rabbit or deer because they belong to the lord and his men will cut my hands off.'

She laughs again. 'They don't come here. And if they did, they wouldn't see.'

'How do you know?' I whisper, fearful that they are at the door.

'Did you see the house yesterday?'

I think about it. No, I did not. I do not know how.

'No, Mother. How did I not?'

'That's for later. Now, you need meat. It'll do you good after what's been happening.'

Slowly, but somewhat less fearfully, I raise a small amount of stew to my mouth. It is the most delicious thing I have ever tasted and I take it down in short time. Mother gives me more, without asking if I want it. I eat it, more slowly, enjoying every wonderful taste.

After the meal, I take the bowls to the pond to wash them. Mother seems to approve that I do not need to be asked. It was my job at home.

Back inside, Mother is watering the plants. She is talking to them as she does so. Perhaps she is mad and that is why I have been sent here. Perhaps the dell is the place where the villagers place their foolish ones. If so, I do not mind being here, or being mad. Mother is strange, but I sense she is good and will treat me well. Perhaps I will live to be six tens and three! But I still do not know why I am here. I think of John the miller and my mother and Mary. Am I to see them again?

Mother beckons me back to the table. She sits opposite me.

'You were sent here because you are like me, lad. Master Thomas does not know what that means, but I have told him to watch out for people who are strange. You saw a man in your room, I hear. And you saw a mist around the stones. Well, I am here to tell you that you are not mad, but you need to understand these things and more.'

I look at her, wide-eyed. Anyone who can tell Master Thomas to do anything is a marvel. I am still afraid, but I also want to know. Can she explain these things? Can she help me understand what has happened to me? Can she help me know that the things I have seen are not from a fool's head? She looks deep into my eyes.

Suddenly, there is a noise outside and I jump up. I recognise the sound. It is dogs fighting. Mother goes outside and I follow, a few paces behind. I do not like dogs. We see them on the path

I followed to the clearing. There is deep, loud growling. They stand on their hind legs, trying for each other's throat. There is blood.

Mother raises one hand. Instantly, they stop. They both hang their heads and whimper. A pause. Then they turn tail and head up the path. I marvel. How did she do that? What did she do?

'How...?' I stammer. She smiles at me and gives me that laugh which I am starting to like.

'You have too many thoughts, boy. And you're frightened.' It's true. My mother says I am afraid of my shadow. 'That's why you see fighting dogs.' I have no notion what she means. How can my thoughts make dogs fight?

'And now I suspect you're wondering how you being afraid and having too many thoughts can make dogs fight out there. It's very simple, really.'

She gives me a long hard look and her expression changes. It becomes stern and has something else in it that I cannot quite place.

'You see, boy, the world is not the way it seems. You and I need to talk so you can understand the way it is.'

We go back inside the comfortable house and sit once more.

Chapter 5

Mother sits me down and places a plant pot in front of me. In it, there is a stem with a beautiful flower.

'So we might as well start. What colour is this?' she asks.

'Blue. Like the sky.' I answer.

'Look again,' she says.

I look again. At first sight, it is indeed blue like the sky. As I look at the edge of the flower, I see white, then streaks of light sun colour and a lighter blue. Deep inside, I see a darker blue with streaks of light red and gold. Suddenly, I find it beautiful beyond words. I feel a tear in my eye.

'Aye, lad, the world is beautiful,' she says, as if reading my thoughts. 'All you have to do is see.'

I always thought the world was ugly and hard and that a short visit to the stone ring, or a crust from John the miller, or a smile from my mother were the few happy things. Perhaps I can find beauty in other places.

'Now listen,' says Mother. 'Where did this plant come from?'

She pauses, but I do not think she means me to answer. I know about seeds.

'This plant came from a seed. But where did the seed come from? From another flower. But how was the flower made? By a bee. The flower gives colour and smell and the bees comes. Bees get dust on their backs. The flower gives it. When they go to another flower, the bees give and the flower receives. Later, the flower gives the seed and the land receives it. The land gives and the seed receives.

'This is how it is, lad. For anything to come into this world, there must be that which gives and that which receives. There are two sides: men and women, hot and cold, light and dark. They come together and new things are made. It is true of us, too. Inside and outside. Above and below. Happy and sad. This world and the other world.'

She pauses, staring at me, not unkindly. She knows I have a question.

'Out with it, lad!'

'Mother, what other world?'

She laughs. 'That's the right question!'

'There is another world, all around us. Inside us too. That's what you saw when you saw the man by your bed. You would call him a ghost, or a spirit, but in that other world, he is as solid as this table. And what you saw around the stones? In that other world, the stones are bigger. You saw something around the stones and around the man. It is around all things. I call that stuff the mist.

'But that world is inside you too. Inside becomes outside. Tell me, do you get afraid?'

'Yes,' I say. Very afraid. Often. Almost always.

'Why?' she asks.

'Because bad things might happen. The world is dangerous. People are dangerous.'

'Think on this: are you afraid because the world is dangerous, or is the world dangerous because you are afraid?'

She is mad, I think. Things come first, then fear. It's clear as the night sky.

'Listen, lad. Here's wisdom. What's inside becomes what's outside. There are no accidents. You have to read the signs sometimes. To read them, you have to know their tongue. The feels you have inside are like water outside. The thoughts you have inside are like the wind outside. And they're like dogs. If your thoughts fight, well, you've seen it. If a lot of people have angry thoughts, or sad thoughts—same thing—you're probably going to get a storm. People oft get afraid or angry for a long time and these feels build up the mist. Mist wants to come down to earth. So if you build up a lot of sad angry mist, you're going to have what you call an accident. It's like a lightning strike.

Accidents? Puh! No such thing.

'But here's more wisdom. You can change what you think and what you feel. And when you do that, you start to change the world out there. You get pictures in your head?'

'Yes, Mother. Always.'

'You need to learn to control them. When you make a picture, it's like this plant. If you leave it alone, it will fade and die. But if you put a strong feel into that thought, you water the plant. You picture people hurting you, mayhap. There's the plant. Then you get afraid. There's the water. And then someone hurts you and you say, "Poor me. Someone hurt me. I must be unlucky."

'Change your thoughts. Change your feels. Change your luck. Make the world the way you want it.'

I think on this. Can it be true? I think on it and my thoughts go away, like an untied boat and I am thinking of all the bad things that have happened. Perhaps I was afraid they would happen before they did. I am suddenly pulled back to shore, because she is speaking again.

'And one more thing. Do you get afraid when you speak to Master Thomas?'

'Yes, Mother. Very afraid.'

'But not John the miller?'

I smile. 'No, Mother. John is not frightening.'

'And why not? I'll tell you. John is not frightened. He is a simple man and knows his trade. He puts his life into making flour. Thomas is frightened. That's why he became so big and strong. That's why he wanted to be head of the village. When you speak to him, you are not frightened at the start, but he is and you feel it. You collect his mist in yours and you believe his feels to be your own. You must get to know what is yours and what comes from outside you. And if it's not yours, you need to get rid of it. I can teach you how to do that. Then you'll only be frightened when you have a reason to be.'

Before I can speak, she suddenly changes what she is talking about.

'Here,' she snaps. 'Feel this flower, but don't touch it.'

Now I think she is mad again. Then she raises her hand and slowly, slowly brings it down towards the plant. She stops, a hand's width away from it.

'Try,' she says. 'Close your eyes. Don't think. Inside, say this: "let me feel where the plant's mist is."'

I close my eyes and try hard not to think. It's not easy. I raise my hand. In my head, I repeat, 'let me feel where the plant's mist is.' I lower my hand, as Mother did.

As my hand comes near to the plant, there is something. There is something there! It is like a soft wall. Suddenly, I see my hand and the plant. But my eyes are closed! For a moment, I see a blue mist around my hand and a soft, red-gold mist around the plant. They mix, the mists around the plant and me. I feel the heart of the plant. And it is as if the plant feels me. All this happens in the blink of an eye. I snap mine open.

'There, lad,' she says softly. 'Your first sight and feel of the real world.' She grins.

I think on this. It was real.

'Now you know the other world is real, you can learn to control it. And that is what you have to do.'

My thoughts drift again. A woman in the village—I think it was Mary's mother—once saw a group of crows. She said it was a sign. I did not understand her. She said that there are signs which mean things. A single crow meant death, she said. I cannot remember what a group meant.

What Mother is telling me seems like that. But more. The village woman said that it means things happen. Mother seems to say that things do not just happen. They are part of each of us.

'When do you wash your body, boy?'

'We jump in the millpond in summer. It's too cold in winter.'

She looks at me, and shakes her head.

'What's inside is outside and what's outside changes what's

inside. If you want a clean mist body, you need a clean flesh body. Tunic off and jump in the pond, now. Off with you.'

I see she is serious. I go outside and pull the rags over my head.

Naked now, I walk into the pond. It is cold, but I am used to hurt. After a time, it feels good. The sun is shining, making golden ripples. I have a strange feeling. I think it might be happiness. No, it is not quite that. It is peace.

I float. The sun warms me. I go down like a duck and touch the bottom. It is not far and I could stand up with my head in the air. I rub my face and my hand comes away dirty. I rub again, then take the rubbing all over me.

I turn and Mother is standing there. She takes my rag into the house. I wait. A few moments later, she brings out something different and lays it on the grass. Then she goes back inside.

I rub a little longer, then float, enjoying the sun.

Stepping out onto the dry grass, I pick up the cloth. It is a new tunic! It is made of soft cloth. I pull it over my head. It is bigger than my old one, reaching almost to my knees. And this one has loose sleeves which reach past my elbows. It might even be warm in winter.

Inside, I thank Mother. She says she is happy it fits.

'You need to go in the pond every morning, when the sun comes up. A clean flesh body will remind you to have a clean mist body.'

She wanders around, talking to her plants.

'Words have power, lad. And gentle words have great power. Words change the air and plants feel it. I don't have to say words, but I need to make a gentle sound and feel kind things. Then the plants grow strong.'

She pours a drink she has made with water from the pond and the plants. It tastes of the forest and is delicious.

'Sleep now.'

She points to the other corner of the house and I see a roll of cloth. I lie down, suddenly tired. I hear the soft sounds of Mother moving around. Outside, the birds become quiet. The forest animals stop moving. The sun goes down.

I sleep and dream of the stone again. I am sitting in the air above it.

Chapter 6

'Time to get up, lad.'

I had the most wonderful sleep of my life. I do not feel tired.

But something is wrong. The sun is not up. Why are we getting up now?

Mother walks outside. There is a very faint glow in the east. Dawn is still some time away.

'Hurry, boy. The mist is falling.'

We go around the pond to the other side of the clearing. The air is chill. We sit on the grass.

The mist falls.

'Look deep, lad. Look into the mist.'

I look. I try not to think. I look in the direction of the stone, but the mist is thick and I cannot see the whole. I am not sure about distance and I start to feel as if it is the beginning of a dream. It is as if the space between me and the stone is like the space between me and the past. Or the future.

Droplets of mist seem to come together. I feel I am in a dream for sure, now. Figures move and shift before me.

From my right, one of the figures approaches me. It is a man. He is tall and has no hair. His face is stern, but kindly, like miller John, but he has no beard. His wears a robe, like a lord, but not like a lord, because he has on only a robe and not a tunic or leg covers or shoes. His shoes are just straps of leather and I can see his feet. I think it might be the man who stood near my bed.

I feel no fear for, although it is real, it is also not real. I sense he cannot harm me, nor would he. He stands beside me.

'Do you seek guidance?' he asks.

I do not know what to say, so I say, 'Yes.'

'What do you wish to know?' he asks.

'I wish to understand what is happening to me,' is all I can think to say.

'Then watch,' he says, and the mists whirl and shift.

I see a church, far bigger than the one in the village. It has a point on the roof and a cross on top. There are more people going in than there are people in the village. The priest looks on. The mist swirls and I see golden ground and nothing growing. Strange beasts walk, like horses with high backs. There are three huge buildings, four-sided, white coloured, dazzling in the strong sunlight. On top of each of the three buildings, there is a point, possibly of glass, with sparks of misty light flying off it in all directions. Men looking like the one next to me are standing in lines as others, in simpler robes, walk towards the huge buildings. One of the men is wearing better clothes than the others. He has no hair on his head, or anywhere else. He appears to have authority. He holds a rough piece of paper and scribbles on it as he stands. He signals to one of the others, speaks a few words to him and the more lowly man nods and heads off to address some others, lower still in rank than himself.

The mist swirls and we are on top of a mountain. A building. Many men in dark gold-red clothes, one arm bare. There is singing and, with the song, the mist in the building swirls in many colours. It is beautiful. The mountains are incredibly high, with snow on them. Birds hop on the rocks, next to the men, as if they are not scared of people. A wind, which I cannot feel, flaps the clothes. It also flaps small pieces of cloth tied to sticks, lining the stone roads. A man looking similar to the one next to me goes inside the building. I am pulled along behind him, like a leaf on the wind when a storm is coming. The man goes into a small room. He sits and starts to sing. I cannot hear him, but I can see the mist swirling around him and taking shape. After a time, a woman appears before him. She is terrifying. She is very tall, has large bunches of hair on the side of her head. Her face is one from my worst dreams. She has large teeth, like a wolf, and her mouth is open as she looks at him, as if she is furious at being summoned. The man continues singing and the woman-beast flies out of the hole in the wall.

The mist swirls and we are in a grassy valley. It is peaceful. A large white building covers most of the valley. Strangely shaped boxes fly through the air. One settles down gently on the white space next to the building. A door opens and two people get out, a woman and a girl. They are clothed in white and smiling. The girl pauses for a moment and looks in my direction. Does she see me? I look at her. She smiles. Then, they step onto a metal circle. Next to it is a box. One of them speaks into the box and they both disappear!

It is wondrous. It is all wondrous. But it is just a dream.

The man raises his hand and the mist settles. I am back with him.

He looks down at me, pauses a moment and then speaks.

'You and you and you. And now...you.'

Then, he disappears.

The mist is gone. I see the stone. I turn, my jaw hanging open and find Mother. She is staring at me, her eyes more piercing than ever. I think that perhaps she is smiling a little.

'Now you must eat. Talk later.'

Breakfast is eggs and bread. I do not know where she got them. Perhaps she went to the village when I was asleep. I am hungry.

After I have washed the plates, I wash myself and put my robe back on.

Inside, Mother is tending the plants. She motions me to sit. She sits opposite me.

'In the land of mist, there is no time. What you saw were different places, aye, but also different times.'

She leans behind her, picks up a plant and holds it in front of me.

'This was once a very tiny seed. Then a shoot grew. Now it is almost full grown. It drops seeds, which fall into the ground and sleep a while. Then they grow and life goes on. What happens when you die, boy?'

I know this one. 'My body will return to the ground. If I am good, my spirit will rest in the house of our Lord forever.'

Mother stares for a moment, then throws her head back and releases a long cackle. She laughs and laughs. She manages to control herself.

'You must find life a bit unfair! All these kings and lords and landowners. And you, a peasant lad with nothing! He-he-he!'

She is right. Life is unfair. Why do I work at a mill and not own one? Why is my mother always so tired from her work? Why do the lords eat deer and rabbits and I do not? And they live in grand houses. I live in a cold room with a goat.

Mother continues.

'You are like the flower, lad. When you die, your body goes into the ground. You got that right. But the thing that is you lives on in the land of mist. Then, like the flower, you come back in a different body. Those people you saw in the stone mist? The man near the tall buildings, the man singing in the mountain room, the girl in the flying box: all you. They are your bodies that were and will be. There are others as well, many others. And every time we come here to this world, we learn something new. This time, you need to know what it is to own nothing. Then you can find the treasure within. When you do that, you will see the treasure that is this world. Do you think, if you were a rich lord's son, you would have found your way here, to me? No. You would be hunting and sword wielding, eating fine food and drinking strong ale and treating poor folk badly. You would not try for a better world.'

Suddenly, I catch sight of something inside me. I see that life is fair. Perfectly fair. Because it looks for balance. You give and receive. You do and have done to you. This is the way of things. Mother does not tell me this, but suddenly I know. This is the truth. But Mother has more to say.

'Those who have been here a few times only, need to learn

about the flesh and things. Food, coin, houses and, he-ha-ha, what they call power! Yes, they are loud and cruel, but they know little about themselves, and nothing about life. But there are others. Old ones. Those who have been here many, many times and know that the flesh world comes and goes. Old ones like me. Like you. We are not important. Well, no more important than the lords and kings. But no less important, either. You remember that! We have different things to learn. The things the rich learn and do affect their lives and sometimes the lives of those around them. But the things we learn to do can change the world. Because the mist world becomes this world. And you can change the mist world here, in this little house in this quiet clearing. Learn to do that and the world out there will become something more than it is.'

As I think on these things, Mother suddenly jumps up and heads for the door.

'Come on! It's time to meet Jack!'

Jack? There is a man somewhere near? I follow Mother, a little afraid. She must feel my mist, because she says, 'Fear not, boy! Jack is good!'

We move round the pond and up a path near the stone. I have not been this way before. It is narrow and overgrown. We walk a short distance and there is another clearing, about three paces across.

Mother sits. I sit beside her. It is quiet. There is no wind. A leaf crackles. A bird, perhaps. The early morning mist is long gone.

'Watch the trees,' says Mother. 'Up there. The leaves.'

I do so, as Mother starts to speak. Or sing. It is all one note, like the monks who came to the village last spring. We had little food, but we gave some to them. They said it was for the poor, which puzzled me, because I had never received food from the monks.

'Mighty Jack, please come to me

And give to us thy blessing three.
I come here with this child of light
To know thy ways and feel thy might.
Jack be nimble, come here now.
Jack be quick, and show us how
To know the ways of fire and air
And water, through thy blessings fair.'

Nothing happens. The air is still. I am not frightened. Mother's song has calmed me.

Then, I see something. The leaves. There is mist around them. The greens shimmer. And I see something. Eyes! Huge eyes, high up in the tree opposite. The leaves below also take shape. They move. A branch and a gathering of leaves become an arm. And another arm. And a man-tree moves into the clearing.

He towers above us. Mother, cross-legged, bends her head forward. I do the same. I am still not frightened.

A voice, which sounds like the wind in a storm and the leaves of the forest and the earth.

'Do you fear me, boy?' it thunders, and yet there is no sound. It is not like listening to a voice, but like a movement in my head.

I dare to look up.

'No, Master, mighty Jack, sir. I do not.'

His leaves rustle, as if in a breeze, but there is no breeze.

'That is well. Nor should you. I am of the forest. I am the forest.'

More movement of leaves and a scratching of the soil.

'What seek you here?'

Mother speaks. 'I introduce this child and ask but for thy blessings three upon him and me.'

'Then it shall be so.'

There is a rustling, as if a storm is coming. Then that voice, at first mighty, is greater still. Jack speaks.

'I greet thee from the forest heart. I am of the earth, but I have the fire of the sun, and the air of the wind and the water of the

32

stream. Be thou blessed by fire, air, water and me, the earth of the land. May growing things be thy domain.'

I feel it! There is fire within me. I am full of ideas. I feel that I can make them be. I feel something I have never felt before. Thoughts rush through my head. I feel full of wonder. There are other feels too. Happy feels. They flow and glow in me. Mother said they were like water! The wind from Jack seems to be inside me and I want to tell the world of these wonders. I feel my feet on the soft grass as if for the first time. The scents of the forest fill me with their sweetness.

I believe I feel the first stirrings of something.

Perhaps it is power.

Chapter 7

I am with Mother by the pond.

'You must learn to love, lad,' Mother says.

I think of my mother. And Mary. And miller John.

'At first, you need someone out there to love. Or something. But if you practise, you can love all the time. Just because you are alive. Learn to love life, lad, in all its forms. Then, nothing can harm you in this world.

'You have choices. You have been frightened a lot. But that was a choice. You can choose to be happy. Or choose to love. It's always in your power. And everyone else's. It's not easy, so you have to practise. Then you'll see the world get better and easier.'

I think on her words. I look at the clearing. The leaves are beautiful. The pond is beautiful. And the stone is, in its own way, also beautiful.

I feel Mother's mist. She is soft and hard. And sparkly, like a damp log on the village fire at the spring dance, when all the married men and women go off to the fields together just before dark. I do not know what they do, but my mother once told me that what they do makes sure we have a good harvest.

Mother is soft and hard. She has fire, but she also has water. She has air, but she also has earth. And these opposite things come together in her. I am starting to love Mother, and she knows it. And I believe that Mother loves me. But she also loves things like the plants she tends. And she loves the wind, she told me, and the rain on her face.

'When you go back to the mist, you take nothing with you but the love you find here. Find things to love, aye, and people if you must. But find the love inside you, lad. Find love.'

Chapter 8

I cannot sleep. It is as if my mist is dancing. Mother snores quietly. I lie still and listen to the forest. I am still surprised I was not fearful of Jack. I somehow knew he was good and would not harm us. I look through the window. Mother has left the shutter open. I see the treetops and, above them the moon. As its light touches me, I feel it, like bathing in the millpond in summer, warm and cool at the same time. As I feel it, I seem to lose myself and float into the mist.

I wake suddenly. It is light outside. Mother is up. She motions me to be quiet.

'Quietly,' she whispers, 'stand by the door.'

I do so. There is a noise outside. Mother goes out, fearlessly.

I look towards the noise. Suddenly, the forest growth opposite from us parts.

Men! Some have swords; some carry staffs. There are dogs.

The one in the finest clothes stops in front of Mother. He has a big sword and an evil face.

'Old woman! Where are the men?'

'No men here, sir. Just me.'

'Why are you here?' he demands.

'Just picking plants for the village. They grow well hereabouts. There's all sorts of...'

'Silence! Where do you live?'

'Live? Why, in the village, master.'

Village? Why does Mother speak untrue? Well, we are so near the village that we are part of it, I reckon. So that is fair.

'Search! Look for men!' he says.

The man walk round the clearing. They will find me. I am not a man, but they often take boys for their fights. That is what this is. They seek men to join them in some war. I think of my father, a distant memory, but still clear. I remember his beard and how

I used to play with it. I remember talk of trouble when he was here and I remember him leaving. To fight yet another war, no doubt.

Do men never tire of war? Do they think they are so different from their enemy? Mother says that, when people, or armies fight, the cause is not their difference, but things that are the same inside them. I think she is right.

They will find me but, strangely, I am not frightened. The men come closer. One looks in my direction. He sees me and the house. But then he looks away again. He returns to his master.

'No men, master,' he says to the bad man. 'Nothing here.'

The master is not happy. Perhaps he seeks men not for himself, but for his lord. There is always someone above us.

'Move on!' he orders. They head back into the forest, away from the village.

Mother turns to me and smiles. She hid me and the house somehow.

She wanders over to me.

'People think they see things, but really they see the mist around things. They just ignore it. If you hide the mist, you hide the things. They still see them, but the seeing does not stay.'

'How do you do it, Mother?'

She sits on the grass next to the pool. I sit next to her.

'Remember, you can change the mist with your thinking. See the stone, yonder?'

'Yes.' Of course I see it. It is important, somehow.

'Close your eyes.'

I do so.

'Now, open them.'

The stone is gone! I look and look in the direction of where it was, but it is not there!

'Now,' she says, 'don't look at the stone. Look at the mist.'

I look, but in the different way I have been taught. There is something in the mist. It is a ball, with a surface like glass. Inside it, I see the stone. I turn off the mist sight and the stone vanishes. I turn it on. It is there.

Mother blinks. The ball disappears.

'Now. You try.'

I try to imagine a ball like the one I saw. It is not easy. I picture it, first in my head, then out there. It takes shape.

'There's the plant. Now, water it,' Mother says.

I try to find a feel, a good one. I remember once playing a game with a bladder full of air. It was such fun. I get that happy feeling and pour it into the ball. It becomes more solid, in the mist world.

Mother seems happy.

'Now. Let it go.'

I do so and the ball vanishes. The stone is there.

'You can put a ball around yourself if you like. Then you can disappear if you need to.'

Chapter 9

I wake with the sun. It is a bad day. I do not know why, but I feel bad. Tired and angry and sad.

I go outside and take off my robe. I dip my dirty feet into the pool. It is cold, but I walk in.

I lie on my back, rising and falling in the water as I take each breath. The sun speckles through the trees. This usually makes me happy, but I am still sad. I do not know why.

I hear Mother. She puts logs on the fire and hangs a pot above it. I rub my feet clean. Then my face and hair.

I feel the sun. Then, with a shock, I realise something. I do not know when we are in the year! I have been here for a long time, but the sun is still warm. How can it still be summer? It should be winter by now, or even spring. Perhaps the seasons do not pass in the clearing, but that does not seem possible.

As I think these thoughts, and as each thought disappears, it is as if they too were made of mist and I forget them. Thoughts of time passing and seasons changing fade away. I cannot hold on to them. They are replaced by a new thought: breakfast.

Mother has mushrooms and bread. She has fried the mushrooms in butter. They are delicious. I wonder about where the bread came from. And I think about Mary. Then I see the day is not so bad.

Mother watches me. She drinks plants in hot water, sipping from the wooden mug, watching me over the top of it as steam rises around her eyes like mist. Outside, I hear a gentle rain, which quickly stops. Rain makes me a little sad.

'Your thoughts and your feels are yours, lad.'

She sips. More steam. A little smile. I hold a mushroom in my spoon, halfway to my mouth. Am I supposed to reply to something so obvious?

I just look at her, a bit sideways, and say, 'Yes, Mother.'

She cackles. When she settles, she sips more plant water.

'Here's wisdom, lad. Most people's thoughts are not their own. Most people have thoughts, but they don't think. When people tell you things, don't just agree with them. Ask yourself, "Is that true?" People hear things and then repeat them as if they were their own ideas. You need to know what it is that you really think. What do you believe? What feels right to you? Your mist body knows all. You need to talk to it. Maybe last night you had a dream you forgot. You woke up grumpy. It happens. Then you get breakfast and you're not grumpy. Then it rains, and you're grumpy again. Then I say something and you feel confused. Then you eat your mushrooms and you're happy. Thoughts and feels blown like a leaf in a wind. Not even a wind, a summer breeze.'

I think about what she says. It seems she is right. I feel foolish.

'What can I do, Mother?'

She smiles. 'Take control. Stop the thoughts. Stop the feels. Then you can talk to your mist. It will tell you things. To hear them, you have to listen and you can't do that if your head is noisy. Your mist body is full of summer light and it will guide you to it. All you have to do is follow. When you catch yourself with a bad feel, frightened, or angry, or sad, then you can rise above it. Look at the thoughts and feels and see them for what they are. Leaves passing in the wind. Let them go.'

I finish my mushrooms, thinking about what Mother said.

I wash the bowls. Mother gives the plants water.

They are growing well.

Chapter 10

I wake with the sun. Mother is up. She has a cloth on the table and is placing things on it. I cannot see what they are. She looks outside, holding her head still, as if listening to the wind. She nods and goes back to placing things on the cloth.

'Time to get up, lad,' she says, without looking towards me.

She takes the corners of the cloth and ties them together. She finds a long stick in the corner of the room and ties the cloth to one end. I stand.

She hands me the stick with the bundle.

'Time to go,' she says.

'Go, Mother?' Is she sending me away? I am frightened at the thought of going back to the village. Then I remember her words and stop myself being frightened.

'Into the forest.'

I wonder what she means. We are in the forest. Well, on the edge of it.

'I have taught you the simple things. Before I teach you more, you must learn to use what you know. Here's what you must do. Go up the trail yonder, then take the main path away from the village. Head towards Dol. After half a morning, there is a huge oak. The path goes to the left of it. To the right, hidden by leaves, there is another path, a narrow one and ancient. Take it for another half morning and you will see another dell, smaller than this one. Stay there for three nights. On the fourth day, return. When you come, you must hold in your hand a wolf, made of wood. There is a knife in the bundle with a little food, but you'll need to find more. Go now.'

I have a lot of questions, but she pushes me out of the door. I put the stick over my shoulder. I turn back to tell Mother I will see her in four days, but she has gone inside.

I step onto the path I took so long ago. When I reach the main way. I look towards the village. It no longer seems like home. I turn right and head into the forest.

The sun is up now, but it is dark in the forest. There are just a few sunbeams where there are not so many leaves. I know the names of all the trees. The way is easy so, to pass the time, I look at the mist around the trees. Some are bright and dancing, others slow and strong. I see my mist joining theirs. It is as if they know me and I them. I feel safe, surrounded by strength and brightness.

I see a mighty oak up ahead. It is huge. Its mist is slow moving, up and down. I see the mist pulling up water and pulling down the fire of sunlight. Fire and water mix in its heart and the tree grows. I stop, place my hands on the tree and greet it. It wraps me in its mist. I feel strong like the tree. Solid. Fire and water mix in me and I know I can create a wooden wolf for Mother.

I move to the right of the tree and part the growth. The leaves are many and strong here, as if they feed off the mist of the mighty tree. After a lot of looking, I find it. The hidden way. It is indeed a narrow path, but one which has been trod by people in the past, for it is clear, now that I see it.

I have a sudden thought that I am alone. For the first time in my life, there is nobody else. Before Mother, I would have been frightened, but now I am not. I head down the path. It narrows and widens, but it is easy to follow. I am hungry, but I decide not to eat from the bundle. I might need it later. I come to a stream. I wonder if it is the one which flows near my home as it is heading towards the village. Here, it is not so wide and I can jump across if I wish. First, I stop and drink. The water is clear and tastes of the forest. It is good water. I put my right leg forward, bend my left leg and jump.

On the other side, the forest is the same, but different. It feels strange. The air is thicker somehow, like in Mother's dell. I raise my mist sight. There are people! Everywhere, I see mist bodies! When I see them, they see me and crowd around. I do not know what to do. If I lower my mist sight, they will still be there. They start to speak. A noise of mist voices, far away and yet very close.

Just as I feel I am going mad, I take control. 'Stop!' I shout. They stop. They stand there, staring at me.

'If you talk one at a time, I will listen. You,' I say, pointing at a young woman.

'Bless you, Master,' she says. "Master"! I try not to smile.

'Where am I?'

'In the forest.'

'How do I get home?'

'Where is your home?'

'Dol village.'

'Why are you here?'

'The world seems clearer here. If I go to Dol, I cannot see it so well. It is too misty. Here, the mist is thin.'

I see she does not know her flesh body has died. How can I help her? I try to remember what Mother told me about people who have passed from life to the other life. I have it.

'Bless you, miss. You have a new home. Do you not remember?'

She looks a little like she is waking from a strange dream. I continue.

'See there. Do you see that light?' She looks up into the trees. 'And do you see the steps leading up?' I help her to make the picture. Mist steps appear and go up into the light. That is the land of mist, where we come from and where we will go. She nods.

'Go up, into the light. Your home is there.'

She looks at me a little uncertain. I smile. She turns towards the light and, slowly, steps up. She turns and looks at me again. I smile and nod. She goes up and disappears in the light.

I turn to the others.

'There is your home. Follow the girl and God bless you.'

They all hesitate. Then one, another and then all of them head up the steps. Just before the steps and the light fade, I think I hear the sound of laughing and rejoicing.

The forest feels lighter and I continue my journey. I think about the lost ones and wonder how long they have been here. She said the mist was thin here. Mother says that there are places in the land where that is true. Her clearing is one place like that, which is why she lives there. Perhaps I am why the mist people were here. They were waiting for someone who could see them. As I walk, I feel I have done a good thing.

The sun is nearly overhead. I must be near. The forest growth thickens and I have to push through leaves to continue. I push aside a sapling and see the dell in the clearing. It is smaller than Mother's, as she said. But it is as beautiful. Just a small dip in the ground, with trees around. There is no house, of course, so I will need to find a place to sleep.

On the opposite side I see a low branch, full of leaves. It will shelter me if it rains. But I think of Mother's clearing and the stone. Perhaps there is a stone here. I raise my mist sight.

The clearing is full of light! It flashes and sparks everywhere. It is beautiful. In one place, there is more, like at the stone. I go to that place and feel myself filling with the light. It is wonderful and I feel strong, even after my long walk.

I sit at the side, near the low tree branch, and open Mother's bundle. I find the knife and remember my task. There is bread and cheese. I pull off a little of each. I do not eat too much, as it will not last three days. I wonder about water and listen. There. That way, there is a small stream. I move out of the clearing a few steps and find it. It is small and there is a tiny waterfall, as high as my knee. I cup my hands and take my fill.

Then I hear a sound. A deep, low growl. Wolf! I stand and slowly back towards the clearing. Then I see it as it approaches me. It is a big one and I feel small. Another step backwards. Is it alone? I look round and listen. Where is the pack? A quick cast around of my mist. There are no others. The lone wolf steps forward again. I gently push my mist towards it. It raises its head, as if sniffing. I take a breath, as Mother taught me, think good thoughts, feel happy feels and, as I breathe out, send it to brother wolf. He hangs his head and becomes soft. I look at him. The mist is red near his front paw. I sit and he slowly walk-crawls towards me. Very gently, I take his paw, feeling kind all the time. I see it. It is a thorn. I hold his paw and pull it out. He yelps, then calms. He licks his paw. Then he licks my paw, the hand that ended his pain.

I go to the clearing. He follows. As I sit, he sits. I have so little food, but I spare him some bread. I do not know if wolves eat cheese. Perhaps some of the carrots Mother has included. I offer him some and he wolfs it down. He lies next to me and I ruffle his fur. I am not alone anymore. Perhaps we are never really alone, even in a dark forest.

Wolf reminds me to turn my thoughts to my task. I do not know why Mother would tell me to do such a thing. I have no knowledge of making things, so perhaps she wants me to use my hands.

I start to imagine how such a thing could be done. Wolf seems to sense that I am thinking of wolves and he looks at me, but not at my face. He seems to look around my shoulders, whining gently. I think that I need to start with a block of wood. I am not sure where I will find one.

I stand and look around. There are a few twigs at the edge of the clearing. I take a few steps into the dark of the forest, never losing sight of the clearing. I find a small log, but it is rotten and crumbles as I pick it up. Near that, there is a larger log, splintered at one end. Perhaps it fell off during a high wind, or was struck by lightning. I pick it up. It is heavy. I believe it might serve, so I carry it back to the clearing.

The air is still warm, so I will not need a fire tonight. I think about real wolves. Will wolf keep them away? Will he tell them I have been kind? I hope so.

I sit with my log. I take the knife and cut off the small twigs.

Next, I strip the bark. I think I should try to cut through it so that I have a round shape. Then, I realise that where the log thins at one end will serve as the nose. Wolf gives a snort as if he agrees.

I start to cut and scratch with the knife. The wood is hard and my progress is slow. I think more about the shape, looking at it from all sides. My hands are rough from the mill, so it is easy to use the knife. I have not done much when the sun starts to go down. I think of sleep.

Perhaps the low-hanging branch is not safe with no fire and wolves about. Again I wonder if wolf will protect me from his brothers and sisters. Perhaps a tree branch. I look up. Most are too high. Some are low, but too narrow to use as a bed. Then I see one. About my height off the ground, wide and with a slight hollow where it meets the trunk. I climb up. Wolf sits on the ground beneath and stretches out. He is tired too. I sit with my back against the trunk. The evening is warm. Although I am tired, I find sleep difficult. I think it is because there is nobody here. I am alone for the first time in my life.

I close my eyes and think about my life and how far I have come since I left the village and met Mother. I truly do not know how long it has been. Then, I wonder what is happening in the village. Has John the miller got a new apprentice? Did the men take any of the villagers, or did Mother persuade them to go in a different direction? And I think of my mother. Strangely, I do not miss her. I think of her with love for giving me life. Life was hard for her and for me, but that is the way of things. Well, it was the way of things, but Mother has taught me that it does not have to be that way.

I sometimes wish I could go back to the village and teach everyone the things I am learning. What a world it would be if everyone thought kind thoughts and pictured good things in their heads, instead of terrors, sadness and anger. Then I realise that they would not listen to me. People are not ready to see things in a different way, even to let go of their misery. One day, perhaps.

A breeze flutters the leaves. It is still warm.

The next day, wolf is gone.

With no people to talk to, I talk to myself. Then I remember Mother talking about my mist body. Perhaps I can talk to it. I do not know how, but I know I must stop thinking and feeling. I close my eyes and turn on my mist sight. The clearing is there before me, even with my eyes closed. It is still full of light. After a time, a figure approaches from my right. It is the same bald man. He smiles.

'Who are you?' I ask with a thought.

'I am part of you. I am here to answer any questions you may have.'

I think for a moment. 'What should I do?'

'That I cannot answer.' he says. 'The decision is yours. But I can help you after you make the decision.'

'Are you my mist body?' I ask him.

'Not exactly, but my answers are its answers,'

I ponder on this. Mother said that we cannot understand the way of mist with our thinking as it is just mist. But we can make a picture with our mind and fill it with mist. That way, it will come to be, in its own way.

'What is this place?' I ask him.

'It is a clearing of power. Many people have come here to learn the ways of the mist. For thousands of years, people have learned the real ways of life in places like this. Where you learn with Mother is another such place. The earth mist has great powers here, just like around the stones in the village.'

I know he is right. I can feel it. But how do people learn the ways of life here if there is nobody to teach them.

I ask him this.

'But there is someone here to teach you,' he answers.

I realise he means him. Or me. Or both of us. Who are both me.

I ask him for wisdom.

'First you receive so you know what to do. Then you imagine it. Then you think how. Then you want it to be. Then you take action. So things come to be.'

I think about his words. It is as Mother says. It is simple and clear.

I thank him and say for God to bless him. He smiles and fades. I open my eyes and look at my block of wood, not yet resembling a wolf. I make a picture in my head of how I would like it to look.

The morning is spent cutting. When the sun is high, I get hungry. I go to the stream and drink from the tinkling waterfall. Then I go a short way into the forest, looking for food. I find mushrooms, but I do not know enough and my mother always told me that some mushrooms can kill you. I find berries and eat. Not the orange ones. They give you pain in your middle. Others can kill you. Nature is bountiful, but also dangerous. I find more berries. The red ones. They are delicious, but I know I must not eat too many.

I turn back. I cannot see the clearing! I think it is this way. I go a few paces, but still cannot find it. I turn my head quickly. Looking, looking. I am lost. Lost in the forest.

In the past, I would have been like the May dance, when the young men run round in all directions, play fighting with each other, wood sword battles, shouting and screaming as the girls sit and watch. Everyone gets hot and then heads for the maypole. The dance is frantic and I can feel it rising inside me. Then I remember Mother. I grow calm, like the clearing pond. I take a deep breath and let it go. I turn on the mist sight and look around. There! A shaft of light. I follow it and, sure enough, there is the clearing.

I take more water and settle down with my wood, which is not yet a wolf head. I carve in the eyes.

The next day, the head is taking shape. I keep imagining a

wolf's head. Changing the solid world is harder and slower than changing the mist world. And it takes time. Pictures in my head take an instant, but making a wolf head will take a long time. Perhaps three days. I continue and, while I carve, I listen to the sounds of the forest. There are birds singing. Small things crawl. It is never silent. After a time, I realise that I have not been having thoughts. Now, I start to think. I think of Mother and what she said about the wolves fighting. When I arrived in this clearing, I was thinking a lot and a wolf appeared. Perhaps wolf has shown me that I can stop my thoughts, even if they are hurting. If I can listen to my thoughts from up above, from the mist land, they are less important and I can control them. Then I can be more clear on what I have to do.

Making the wolf is so hard. If I had not spent so much time carrying for miller John, my hands would be soft and it would be more difficult. I am suddenly angry at Mother. She sent me away into the forest and gave me a pointless task. I throw the partly made wolf head down and stand up. I run to the other side of the clearing, shouting. The forest goes silent for a moment, then resumes its chatter. As I shout, I feel something in my middle. It is not like a normal shout, where my middle goes tight. Something stirred. I stop. I feel. I look around at the trees. After a time, I see a bird. I wonder. Trying hard to get the same feeling in my body, I speak to the bird.

'Brother bird. Fly to that branch,' I say, pointing to another tree.

It sits there, singing. I try again.

'You. Bird. Fly over there.'

It flies! As I marvel, I want to talk to Mother about it, but she is half a day away, so I talk to myself. I see the responsibility I have. I decide to call this my voice of power. I know I must use it wisely.

I return to my carving and another day passes.

The next day, the head is looking more and more like a wolf.

I have drawn the knife in lines down the neck and lifted the lines a little to show the fur. The teeth are difficult and I worry about breaking them. As I continue to cut and scrape, I start to wonder when it will be finished. I set it down and look. It looks like a small wolf's head. I could do more, but I know that things in the world are never perfect. It is not perfect, but I have to decide if it is as good as it can be. I believe it is.

I take the wolf's head to the stream and wash off the wood chips. It is quite a bright colour, so I look for something to make it darker. I find some plants with dark roots. I collect two small stones and place the roots between them. After a time, I have dark root water. I use my fingers to spread it on the head. There is not enough, so I grind more. I think of John the miller and his great stones. Would he be proud of me?

I do not spread the juice everywhere on the head, but leave some parts light, as if daylight was shining on its fur. I leave it to dry in the sun and sleep.

I dream I am flying over the forests of the world, past high mountains, over wide rivers. For one moment, as I fly alongside some geese, I think I see, in the far distance, a huge village. I fly towards it, but wake up.

It is dark, so I climb up to my branch. Tomorrow, I am going home.

The next day, I wake just before the sun. I sit on my branch and watch the light creep into the world. I am reminded of the wolf and how his growl was calmed by the light of the happy mist I sent forth. The world needs light. It needs the light of the sun, but it also needs the light of the mist, sent forth by everyone. As the land of mist becomes this world, there must be light up there before it can be down here. I summon the light inside me.

I am not afraid anymore.

I collect the wolf's head and place it in the cloth, alongside the knife. I slip it onto the stick and set off. As I walk through the forest, I hear the sounds again. When I was coming here, I was afraid of wolves. Now, I am not. They can come and I can make them my friends. I know that the world can still hurt me, but it will not be because of what I think and feel. Now, I am not afraid of people, either. They are more afraid than I am. As I grew in the village, they made me afraid of the things they were afraid of. Now, I know these fears for what they are.

The walk is wonderful. Sunlight spots dance on the leafy ground as the treetops sway in the gentle breeze. It is warm and a forest-scented breeze tickles my face. I love the smell of the forest. My bare feet find their way and I feel like I am part of the forest.

I reach the mighty oak and turn left. The journey seems much faster than when I came here.

When the sun is almost overhead, I spot the narrow way to Mother's clearing. She is there, waiting for me.

'Your mother is dead,' she says.

Chapter 11

I am still a young boy. I am sad, but I try to rise above the sadness and see it for what it is. It is just change. Life is change. It is natural. Mother comforts me.

'This is a big lesson, lad, and a hard one,' she says. 'All things come and go. Now, though, you know that you will see her again.'

I think of the people lost in the forest. Perhaps my mother is lost, too. I tell Mother this.

She seems to drift off. I know what she is doing. I try to raise my mist sight too, but I cannot.

'There! There she is! She is looking at you! She is smiling. She is sad that she was not able to do more for you, but she was always so tired. She is not tired anymore. And she is sad that she could not say goodbye. But she is smiling and so happy. She is happy that she is going home and she is happy for what you are becoming. There! She sees the light. She walks towards it. She stops. A last look at you. She smiles. She loves you so much. You are her baby boy. And she's gone. The light fades. It is done.'

I cry and cry and cry. Mother holds me.

Later, I sit gazing at the calm water. The sadness goes as I put it in its right place. The world has turned. It is different, but the same. A new life for me. Mother knows.

'There, lad. You know it is the way of things. Mostly, we are sad for ourselves when someone leaves us. Especially you and me, because we know they are well and happy. We are without them and must continue, so we feel sad for a time. But the only way we can change this world is by being in it.'

I think about her words. We do not have to do much, but we have to think and feel in a good way. And make happy pictures in the mist. I try to let my mother go and start to imagine the future.

'Mother, what's to become of me?' I ask.

'You will know, when the time comes. For now, we must go to the village. It is blessing time.'

I am about to ask her what that means, but she is up and in her house, collecting plants and potions. I realise she didn't ask me about the wolf's head.

It feels strange as I walk behind Mother, back to the village... back to my home, which is no longer my home. We cross the field, and as we reach the path, I glance up the hill towards my old house. It must be empty now. I feel a little sad, but I smile. We head down the path, past Mary's home. I do not look for her.

In the field with my ring of stones, there is a bone fire burning. All the village is gathered.

Men line the way on either side, and Mother and I walk between them, towards the fire. The sun is going down and I see Long Hec, the biggest stone, dark against the setting sun. Master Thomas steps forward. I remember my old fear at seeing the head of the village. Now, I am not afraid.

'Greetings, Mother. Greetings, young Master.' He bows slightly at us in turn. I marvel at this, but keep my breath moving steadily.

'Blessings on you, Master Thomas, and on the village,' Mother says.

She heads towards the stone ring. Mother stands me in front of Long Hec. She tells me to be open to the mist when it comes and to let it go out into the village. I turn on my mist sight and see it gathered around the stones. There is more where I stand, as Long Hec seems to gather it from the other stones.

Mother opens her bag and starts to walk in a circle, just inside the stones. She is muttering something, but I cannot hear it. She stops at each stone, says a few words and dabs some plant juice on them. As she does so, each stone lights up. When she reaches the last stone, next to me, she pauses and looks at me. 'Ready, lad?' I nod.

She touches the final stone. Nothing happens. Then she steps into the centre of the circle. She holds one arm out, pointing to the stone on my left, then the other arm, pointing to the one on my right. There is a shift in the mist air. A sound starts, deep and of the earth. Each stone lights up around the circle. The power builds and it starts to move around the circle, slowly, slowly. Finally, it reaches Long Hec. And me.

All the power of the stones and of the light and of me shatter the air. I let it flow through me. It is almost too much for me, but I breathe and let it go with each out breath. It flows into the circle, but the circle cannot contain it and it shoots out into the village and the forest and the farms and over to the mill and the dairy. In the heart of the light, a figure appears. A mighty warrior, clothed in strong leather armour, but not one I have seen before. He has a huge beard and scars on his face. He has a face of power but it is not unkind. He sees me.

'I am Ulph!' he thunders. 'I offer my blessings and protection.'

I feel I must reply. 'I greet thee, mighty Ulph, and give thanks and blessings from this world.'

I see by his slight smile that I have replied well. He raises his arms and more light comes. It passes through the stones, through Long Hec and through me. It feels different. It has a strength. Somehow, I know the village will be safe for another year. Ulph fades away and the light fades with him. As it goes, I see the villagers look on and I realise they have seen nothing.

'It is done,' says Mother to Master Thomas.

Mother moves towards me and catches me, for I am about to fall. I gather myself and stand upright. She mutters to me quietly, 'You have Ulph's blessing. It is well.'

I whisper back, 'Who is he, Mother?'

'He was the first dweller in the clearing. He stays to help protect the village. We owe him much.'

I nod.

She turns towards Master Thomas and raises her voice. 'Is

there no food and drink for a tired old woman and a hungry boy?'

Master Thomas bellows with laughter and the villagers join in.

We go to Master Thomas's hall. The feast is a marvel. I am sat at the top table with Mother, Master Thomas and some of the village elders. There is meat and cheese and beer, even mead. I am happy.

When the dancing starts, Master Thomas turns to Mother and asks about me. 'How is he shaping?'

'He's good. Almost there. Just one more task and then he's done.'

Master Thomas smiles and relaxes. He drinks more beer.

The noise and drinking stop as Mother rises. The villagers watch in silence as she makes her way to a chair which has been placed in the centre of the hall.

Mother goes silent and breathes deeply. She closes her eyes. Quietly at first, she starts to speak.

'This coming year will be a good year. The crops will be good, the weather kind. The village will thrive and the lords will take no more than last year. Your kindness to each other is important. There may be a little snow, but it will not be a hard winter. But bring in plenty of logs. Keep the fires burning. Set aside meat and salt the fish as usual, and…'

She stops. There is a soft murmur around the room. She continues.

'Men are coming. Not next year, nor the year after, nor the year after that. But in a few years, men are coming. They have pointed heads and come from across the sea. Their bows are not like ours. They hold them flat, not upright. They have swords and clothes of metal. They come! They take our land. All of it. They take all the animals. Men are killed for eating deer. They take taxes when the people have nothing. They will keep our land for over a thousand years. Then we will get it back, when the time of the spirit starts to return. All things pass. It gets harder. Buildings are built higher. Everything seems easier, but men still toil. I cannot see. There is a darkness over the land. People have things, but they are not happy. They have food, but they are still hungry. I cannot see. I cannot...'

She fades out and wakes from her travels.

'A little beer, I think,' she says.

The revels are over. People go home and we are left alone with Master Thomas.

'It is not good, Mother,' he says.

'No, Thomas. It is not, but it will pass. The biggest feel I got was not that they will take our land, but that they will take our spirit. They want people to think that the world we can touch is the only thing there is. They will come for people like me. They will say the stars do not speak and that mist is not real because you can't touch it. They are fools, but clever fools. When they come, we must say, "yes, master," but stick to the old ways.'

Master Thomas thinks on that, not knowing what to say. He always seemed wise to me. He does not seem so wise anymore. Mother continues.

'I am old and will leave soon. The ways must continue. He is our hope for the future.' She looks at me. Master Thomas nods.

'Come, lad,' she says. 'We must go back. You have a big task tomorrow.'

Chapter 12

Back at the clearing, we eat and sleep.

The next day, when I rise with the sun, it seems brighter than usual. I still do not know the season. It should be late summer because of the blessing, but it is warm. Perhaps it really is autumn and the warmth has stayed longer this year.

We break our fasts on mushrooms, eggs and hot plant drink. Mother seems dreamy. I wash the bowls and myself. The pool is wonderful today in the warm sunshine. Afterwards, I pull on my tunic—it is a new one, given to me by Master Thomas—and my first pair of shoes. They are but flat pieces of leather with thin straps to tie them. I do not like them and take them off. It is not that they are not good shoes. They are. But I do not like something between me and the land. I need to touch it. My feet are hard from a lifetime of being barefoot and I like it that way.

Mother says that one day soon I will make seed. I do not know what that means. She says I might start to like a person in a big way. I do not know what that means, either. She also says that with the seed comes power and I must use it well. She says I will know what to do when it happens.

She takes me outside and we sit, watching the sunrise over the treetops. I think back to what Mother said to Master Thomas... that 'the world we can touch is the only thing there is.' I think it is stupid and cannot believe that people will ever think that. Look at the world! It is alive with light! It connects us all. We are the trees and the stones and each other. How can people believe we are separate? It is madness!

Mother senses my mood.

'Aye, lad. The world is mad. People are born wanting to love, then they forget how. They spend the rest of their lives trying to remember. We are born to love! And the One, the begetter of all mist and all things, wants nothing but to love. That love can come in as many ways as there are people. When your seed comes, you might love a girl, or a boy, or both. It is no matter. When it comes down to it, love is the only thing there is. You've felt it, here in the forest. It was love that made you help those lost people find their way back to their mist home. It was love that made your wolf, which I have yet to see! And it is love that kept you here, when you wanted to go back to the village, back to your mother. Love is all, boy. Remember that.

'When the men come from across the sea, you must hide, deep in the forest. Keep alive the knowledge I've taught you. Practise the chants, talk to the forest god. He will keep you safe. When you are older, you must find another to teach. Promise me, lad. This must keep going. When you teach, you will use your own story. You will add to what I've said. That has always been the way of things. In other times, in other places, they had other words and other stories, but the heart of the story is always the same.

'Now, you have one final task before I send you on your way. Show me your wolf.'

Send me on my way? What does she mean? Am I to leave her? Mother says nothing more. I go into the house and into the corner where I sleep. There, I find the wolf's head, wrapped in Mother's cloth, untouched since I returned from the other clearing. I take it outside and set it in front of Mother.

She smiles and picks up the cloth. Gently. With respect. Slowly, she unwraps it. As she takes it in her hands, I hear her gasp. A tear comes to her eye. I have never seen her like this. She looks through her tears at me.

'It is beautiful!' She cries, unable to contain her feels. I smile, but I am suddenly shy. I see the wolf's head for the first time since I returned. I must own it is good. The light catches it and the scrapes and root paint show the fur. The eyes seem to look at me.

'This object, made by your own hand, will bring you back

here when you fly. And fly you will. Hold it, lad. Tonight you sit on the stone.'

The stone! It has fascinated me since that first day I spent alone here. I have not dared to sit on it. The mist is so strong there, even more so than at Long Hec. What will I feel when I sit upon it? Will I be able to let it pass through me? Should I even try, or should I let it fill me. I ask Mother.

'It will fill you, aye, but you cannot contain it all. Nor can you let it all pass through you. All you can do is let it lift you up. Breathe and follow where it takes you. First you must rest. You will sit on it as the sun sets.'

I have trouble resting. When the sun is above us, mother gives me a drink. She says I can have no more food today, as then I will be too heavy for the mist to lift me. She says that later, she will give me something special to drink.

I rest in the afternoon sunlight. I close my eyes. When I open them, the sun is low in the trees. I must have slept, but I did not dream. Mother is standing above me.

'Come, lad,' she says, gently.

We go inside and she sits me down. She holds up a cup.

'This is a plant drink, but not like you have had before,' she says. 'You will fly. Remember to breathe and keep hold of your wolf's head. When you get back, I will be here.'

I drink the water. It is bitter. We stand and Mother embraces me. She leads me to the stone. I feel the same, but different somehow, as if I am not quite on the ground. The grass is soft and cold beneath my feet, yet not quite there.

I approach the stone and keep breathing. I feel the power coming off it. Mother looks into my eyes. 'Remember, I'll always be with you.'

She turns and goes back inside.

I sit on the stone, then lie down. I look up at the blue, blue sky, the colour starting to fade. It is beautiful.

Suddenly, without warning, everything goes white. Bright,

brilliant, blinding white. Within the white, there is more. An even whiter white flashes and burns. I grasp the wolf's head, but it is as if these are not my fingers. Then, I soar upwards. I feel like a spring bird. It is terrifying. It is marvelous.

I fly through the white. Then, I am somewhere else. Men of stone tower above me. A man stands with his back to me. He has no hair. He wears a long robe and sandals. There is sand everywhere.

He turns and looks at me. He blinks and I am inside him! No, I *am* him. I just know that I am looking at the mist shape of a boy in a short tunic. He is barefoot and looks so young. I dismiss him from my mind.

I turn towards the temple. The ceremony is about to begin. As we process inside, the others line the way and bow as I pass. Inside, the gods look on from their stone homes. The animal gods of this great land. I begin to chant and the others join in. It took me three moons to write the ceremony. Care is essential as so many things can go wrong. Every word is precisely the right one. There is no allowance for error. At the first mention of the god's name...

...I am outside once more, gazing up at the huge building and statues. A boy once more. I start to panic, but I breathe and think of Mother's teachings. The sun beats down. There is gold everywhere. Children race between the buildings, but are chased away by a tall man with a long staff. And I fly...

...over the buildings, across a vast river, over the sea and hills and valleys. I am wondering how I will get back to Mother, when I find myself on rocks before a huge building, impossibly high. It must have tens of tens of rooms. I look around and see mountains. Huge mountains with snow. A wind comes up the valley and flutters the tiny cloths on the sticks by the side of the path which leads to the building. There are people, some with animals I have never seen. I move towards the building. It is not like walking. It is like being a blade of grass, drifting on the millpond.

The people have dark skin, with lines. I suppose the wind and the dust darken the skin and that the lines are caused by closing their eyes against the sun, which is strong and bright here in the clear sky.

Inside the walls, in a yard, a man stands. He nods to all the people coming in. He sees me! He looks at me and smiles. It is a kindly smile. I think I smile back, but I have little control over my mist body. He turns and opens a door. Inside, there are steps. He closes the door behind him, keeping the people out and...

...I climb the steps, and more steps, and more. I enter a room. It is small. Something is burning in a dish, giving off thick smoke. Lamps, containing some sort of oil, burn on all four sides of the room. Three men, dressed like me in gold-red robes, right arms bare, sit on three sides. I take the fourth. I nod three times. We all start chanting together. It is low, very low, and yet there are incredibly high notes soaring above the low ones. I feel the vibration in my throat. The room takes on a strange quality, as if it is not quite here. Outside, the mist rolls down the mountains. Huge, and very strange, figures pass through the room. One is mighty, and powerful. It turns to me and...

...I am in the yard again, looking at the closed door. Suddenly, once more, I am a bird. I fly down the mountains, into the valley, past tiny villages, over huge forests, down hills to another tall building. It is pure white. Great columns hold up the roof. Words in a strange language, with strange letters, and yet I can read them. I forget them instantly. There is a woman, dressed in white robes. She beckons her sisters forward, into the great building. And I am her. I feel the weight on my chest. I know things, more than most women, more than all men. I am the goddess. I am the giver of life. I am the one who comes in the night. I am many and all women are me. I feel...

I do not know...who...I...AM...!

...like flying. Straight up into the stars. But I swoop down like that spring bird. Other mountains. More rocks. A calm, clear lake. Thunder rolls around the mountainside. Lightning flashes. There is a man with a huge beard. He holds a hammer. It looks so heavy and yet he is so very strong. As I watch, he takes on the appearance of another. Perhaps a god. A mighty, blond-haired god. He smashes the hammer down and rocks splinter. I become him. I feel his power. I hold the hammer up and shout my thanks. All the long-haired, bearded men shout their thanks too. Fires burn on the hillside. Water trickles down the cliffside into the lake and a wind picks up, rippling the surface. I look at the fires and see tiny fire creatures dart this way and that. I turn to the lake and see liquid creatures, swimming like tiny fish, and yet they are not in the lake so much as they are the lake itself. I leave him and fly again…

…thinking of Mother, thinking of my wolf's head. I cannot grasp it, for I cannot feel my hands. I fly once more. Across the sea. Past land on my left and a huge rock on my right. I turn, as if drawn on by something. The sea flashes beneath me. It is breathtaking. I am faster than any bird. Over land once more.

There are wide paths beneath me. Metal boxes move rapidly along them. I feel I am losing my mind. I am just a boy with no family, who lives in a forest with Mother and who knows the true ways of life. I do not understand these things. This is too much. More buildings. There are too many. They are too high. They must fall! And people. More people than I have ever seen before. More than I can count.

I am losing my mind! I am falling! Falling! Mother!

And I woke up in bed in my flat in south London, sweat pouring off me.

I remember when the fever started. I had just finished work and was on my way home. I didn't feel well, in one of those odd ways where you are not quite sure what is wrong, but you know something is. I started to feel so hot that I thought I was going to have to get off the underground train to get some fresh air. I stuck it out, though, and reached my station. I picked up some food from the supermarket on the way home, just something I could throw in the oven.

I remember I considered phoning my boss to say I probably wouldn't be in the following day, but realised he would have gone home by then. I ate a little, but was not really hungry, which was most unlike me. I felt strange, so decided to have an early night. I slept for ten hours. Normally, I manage six.

The next day, I was sweating and aching. So that's it, I thought: it's flu. In June, for heaven's sake. I made some tea. I was going to have a shower and get dressed, but I was weak, so I knew I wasn't going anywhere that day. After a few minutes, I went back to bed.

Just after nine, I rang my boss, Matt, and explained the situation. He's pretty good, and knows I'm generally reliable, so he told me he'd see me when I was better. I finished my tea and lay back. I glanced at my watch. It was twelve minutes past nine.

Almost instantly, I was asleep again. I woke with the sun, a goat snorting at the other end of the room. That was how it began. I was a boy in what was probably the eleventh century. It seemed to last for months.

When I woke, it was some time before I was certain who I was. The whole thing had been so vivid and coming back to the real world had been so disorientating. I remembered the villagers and the smells of the forest. I remember my mother and my terror when speaking to Thomas. And yet, here I was. In London. I found myself thinking fondly of Mother. It had, as I said, seemed so real.

I had no explanation for it. Of course, it would have been easy to dismiss it as a dream, but it was too vivid for such a simple explanation. What was it, then? I've heard of something called 'astral travel,' where some part of us, our consciousness, can leave the confines of the physical body and travel anywhere in the world. Perhaps my astral self had travelled in time, too. However, I have always been a practical person and have seen no evidence of non-physical realities. The other explanation I had was that someone had slipped something into my coffee at work, some hallucinogen, which had slowly kicked in on the journey home and took hold when I fell asleep. Of these possibilities, I thought that perhaps the last one was the more likely. But I have no idea who would have done such a thing, or why. If someone at work was into drugs, it strikes me as a bit of a waste to use a pill to play a bizarre trick on a colleague.

When the dream, or whatever it was, had finished and I woke up, I glanced at my watch. It was just after eleven o'clock. I assumed I had slept all day and all night, or even for several days. After all, the events in ancient times had gone on for months. Perhaps I was sicker than I'd thought. I picked up my phone and rang Matt, apologising for not having phoned sooner, but I was really sick and had been out of it for days. He paused, before telling me that I'd already rung him that day, two hours earlier. Two hours! That whole thing had taken place in two hours!

That was the most alarming thing. It felt like months. Was that Mother woman right? Was that one of my past lives? Such things are so against modern, Western thinking. And yet, I cannot explain it. As I lay in bed, I even tried to open my mist sight. Nothing happened, of course, but it gives an idea of how real the whole episode had seemed to me.

I was still sweating, so I knew I needed liquids. I managed to walk to the kitchen to drink water and make more tea. I took the glass and mug back to bed with me. I was still weak and sweaty. I drank half the tea and felt sleepy again.

The fever wasn't over yet.

PART II

Chapter 1

The scooter lands and we step off. As we walk towards the pad, I spot a boy in the spirit world. He is wearing clothes from an early age. He is barefoot and dirty. He sees me. He looks nice and I wonder if he is alive now, on one of the other, less-developed worlds, someone who has happened to find himself here. I give him a quick smile. I see spirits a lot and am probably going to join the seers when I am older.

I consider mentioning the boy to Jula, but decide not to. She knows I have sight, like she does, and I have often told her of spirit sightings before, so it would probably not interest her.

We step onto the pad. Jula says, 'Learning room seventy-three,' and, with a flash, we are there.

Some girls have a male guide, but I knew I would be happier with a female one. Jula and I chose each other quite quickly.

Jula and I have planned my learning together. There are so many things I want to know. Of course, I don't see her every day, as she has things to do and I have tasks to perform. But we meet every few days and she guides me towards being me. Like every young one, I want to understand the modern world, but I am not sure of where my love lies yet. Jula and I think that one of the best approaches to understanding the world today is to first learn how things came to be the way they are. So today is history and, I must admit, I am excited.

In Room 73, there are the usual terminals and comfortable chairs. There's a food machine which I'll probably make use of later. Jula tells me that history takes time to learn and I might have a lot of questions.

Jula asks if I want a drink before we start, and I opt for water. She tells the food machine and a glass of chilled water appears. It's a warm day, so cool water is very welcome. We settle ourselves on the chairs and Jula addresses puter.

'Puter, tell the story of the significant events over the last two thousand years. Make the story suitable for this girl.'

Puter says, 'Ready.' It is the voice I chose some time ago, that of a friendly girl.

Jula says, 'Begin.'

The puter voice starts. Occasionally, as it speaks, holo-images appear.

'The first major event,' says the puter voice, 'was the War in the East. Around twenty-eight million people died during the conflict and two hundred million in the ten years following it. As a result of this war, all nuclear weapons were banned in every county in the world. As in all wars, advances in science, technology and medicine happened very quickly. The most significant was the radiation cure, which developed into the cure for all forms of cancer, which was a deadly disease at that time, and the invention of the first hover scooter.'

I say, 'Wait.' Puter stops. 'What caused that disease?'

'Cancer had many forms and many causes. One was radiation from atomic weapons. It was this cause which drove the search for the cure. The most important other causes were the consumption of meat from dead animals, chemicals used in growing plants and carbon emissions from vehicles and factories. However, the most significant factor was a weak immune system due to poor education and stifled emotional expression.'

This is interesting. I never knew people used to eat animals!

'And what were...nuclear weapons?'

'They were war devices designed to kill millions of people and cause enormous destruction of cities. There was much discussion about whether they should be used or not. One problem was that their effects were not localized. Radioactive dust could spread on the wind and in the water. What people did not know was that there had to be specific things happening in the spirit world for them to be used at all. Because of the growing anger amongst the populations in many parts of the world, enough energy built up in the non-physical realm to enable their use. In the war in the east, only three were used, and although the immediate effect was that twenty-eight million died, contamination of food and water led to another two hundred million losing their lives. That was somewhat unexpected by the politicians, and the rage of the survivors led to all such weapons being banned worldwide. They were never used again.'

I had a strange feeling for a moment. I think it was sadness and I had to stop myself imagining the destruction. I turned my feelings to the positive present, as I have done all my life. After all, being able to do that is the main reason we have such a wonderful world today.

'Continue, ' I say.

'The next significant event was the near destruction of the world by artificial intelligence. Several other planets were destroyed in this way. On Earth, more and more devices were becoming connected and the network was allowed to become more and more autonomous. Control gradually slipped away from humans, but they did not see this as a problem until it was too late. As programmers, and later hackers, tried to regain control of things, the network became increasingly sophisticated in preventing what it saw as attacks. Eventually, the network decided that the best way to prevent more attacks was to eradicate the cause. The first human killed by the network was Thomas Dunne in the western megalopolis. He was a systems upgrader working for an insurance company. He was trying to open the door to his car, which the network had locked to prevent him travelling to his job, which involved, as the network judged it, interfering in its existence. His job involved travelling to different branches of the insurance company which he worked for in order to install new hardware and software. His death was at first thought to be a freak accident, as was the non-operation of the carpark security video, until video footage taken by a passer-by emerged later showing the driverless car crushing him against a wall.'

'Wait. Define "hacker".'

'A hacker was a puter expert who accessed password-protected systems illegally.'

'Define "insurance".'

'Insurance was a form of gambling in which people bet an event would happen and others—the insurance companies—bet it would not. If it happened, the gambler would receive compensation.'

'Puter, remind me to discuss this further when you have finished the history. I want to know what you mean by "bet" and "compensation". Continue.'

'Seven...'

'Wait. Puter, how many people lived on the Earth at this time?'

'The population was approximately nine billion, all terrestrials.'

I gasp. I cannot imagine so many people.

'Continue.'

'Seven highly skilled hackers from around the world arranged to meet. The message confirming the meeting was the last message the network allowed. The seven travelled by horse and on foot. One used a camel for part of her journey, another a rowing boat for part of his. The meeting took place underground in an abandoned school. The sealing of the room was the first priority. Then, the Group of Seven worked day and night for seventeen days. Their aim was to regain control of the network. After seventeen days, they had produced the Universal Limiter. They scattered, each possessing a copy of the device. They had to insert a minimum of two devices into the network. Three of the Seven were killed within a day, when the network detected the microprocessors in the devices and it was unable to access them. Another was killed two days later trying to insert the device into a car. The remaining three inserted the Limiter into the network within a minute of each other at different locations throughout the eastern world. The network attempted to destroy the device, but the Seven had devised it in a way that any such attempt would add to the limiting effect. The entire global network was taken control of within three minutes. From then on, no person could be harmed by any device. In fact, the network devices had to ensure the safety of people at all times. Several hundred Universal Limiters were produced, and were installed all over the world. In total, in the twenty-three days since Dunne's death, 7.04 billion people were killed by the network.'

I gasp again. So many.

'How did the survivors manage to live after such loss?'

'It brought people together physically and emotionally, so they comforted each other. Many people at that time still relied on religion for solace.'

I think I've heard of that. In a discussion Jula and I had about the development of the spiritual life around the world, I'm sure she mentioned it as being some sort of spiritual story.

I want a clear definition, so I ask, 'Puter, what is "religion"?'

'Religions were myths people told about the operation of spirit in the world and in themselves.'

'Tell me a little more about them.'

'Religions existed all over the world. They were essentially similar stories, but how they were told depended on the local culture, history and climate. They provided comfort for many millions of people who were, as yet, unable to grasp the concept of a source of all things, which was manifesting in the physical world. People created gods and goddesses as personifications of aspects of spiritual power. For example, thought processes and communication were symbolised, in some cultures, by a God with wings, flying through the air and carrying messages; the spiritual connection which exists inside all people was often symbolised by a God come down to Earth, and so on. They were very well-structured stories, written by people of great spiritual knowledge and experience, and the stories told of a central character's journey through life toward a spiritual awakening. Problems with religion arose because people took the stories literally and believed the characters had actually existed. They probably had, but they missed the point of the stories: it was not so much the people themselves and what happened to them which were important so much as the stories which grew around them. These stories were not about the central character of the religion: they were about everyone. A further problem arose when people began to live their lives according to the story and not according to what the story symbolised. That led to people declaring that the gods in their local story were better, or more important, than the gods in the religions of other countries. Instead of seeing what connected them, people saw what divided them.'

'Wait. So people had no connection to spirit at this time?'

'A few did, and tried to show the followers of religions that their belief was good and useful, but not the whole story. At one time, several movies — forms of audio-visual storytelling for entertainment purposes — told the same story, although many did not recognise the similarities. Religious wars went on for many centuries. Paradoxically, the beliefs which were intended to unite people, so that they could have more peaceful lives, actually separated them, and it was not until there was peace in the physical world, and certain worldly events brought people together, that people started to realise how religion was intended to operate.'

'Interesting. Continue.'

Puter goes on. 'The next significant event, which incidentally began to have an impact on religious belief, was the revelation that there was life elsewhere in the galaxy. The first visitors who revealed themselves to the majority of people were a joint delegation from Alpha Centuri and Tau Ceti. This came as a huge shock to most people, but the existence of extraterrestrials had been known for some time to a small group of people. These wealthy terrestrials had bases on other planets and provided rogue alien planets with minerals and human slaves in return for advanced technology. The first delegation revealed these activities to the world at large. For a short period, once the initial shock had faded, all aliens were regarded as evil, but then the Tau Cetians provided humanity with the first healing devices. Overnight, almost all fatal and debilitating human diseases were eradicated. The Tau Cetians also helped to raise human consciousness, emphasising the importance of this in combating disease. They encouraged people to be kinder to themselves and to other people. Eventually, people realised that there were two types of alien alliances: those who supported humankind in its evolution and those who wanted to limit it and enslave the planet. Prior to the first contact with humans, a galactic war had been won by the alliance of spiritually positive races. They ceased all contact with the rogue planets and placed a protective energy barrier around the Earth to prevent them from visiting again.'

I ask, 'What about the Andromedans and Sirians?' I have a lot of young friends from these places. I met them during the many off-world youth camps I have attended.

'They came later and were also involved in helping to raise human consciousness. Eventually, they took on the training of an increased number of psychic children. They are very advanced civilisations, and although they approved of contact with the human species, they were not involved until later. They felt that their approach to life would initially have been too much of a psychic shock to most human beings. As you know, they are highly telepathic sensitives and humans were not ready for all their thoughts and feelings to be known. After a few generations, when psy children were more common, and their control of their inner worlds were more established, the Andromedans deemed it safe to visit. Initially, they established contact with young children, who found them fun and, in turn, the Andromedans and the Sirians developed a deep respect for the human race, realising that their basic nature was reflected in the children and that the adults had not had the guidance and training they were able to offer the children. In evolutionary terms, the brief period that the Andromedans were here was key to the greatest period of growth in human history.'

This is interesting. I assumed that psys were always here on Earth. Perhaps they were, but were not acknowledged. I can see how their presence would have been a threat to power.

'Continue.'

'The contact with alien species led to one of the most significant steps in evolution: the abolition of countries and governments.'

'Wait. Explain "countries" and "government".'

'At that time, the world was portioned into areas called countries. Each country had its own government. These were people who were in charge of the country. They made laws, which were rules people had to follow, and they hired organised groups of people, such as the police and non-government lawmakers, who forced people to obey the laws. In most countries, people were able to form a government if more people voted for their group than voted for the groups with different ideas and ideals. People did this willingly, because they did not understand their own creative abilities. It was simply easier to give responsibility for creation to other people, even if they didn't like what they created. People were kept in ignorance of how creation happened by their limited education, which focused on the physical world. Daydreaming, imagination and a positive attitude were ridiculed. For the majority, there was no connection with spirit, so people felt lost and unhappy, which made it easier for governments to get the support of the ignorant.'

'Stop!' I say. I have to ponder this. It must have been so lonely to live without spirit. I am still becoming familiar with the physical world, of course, but I am guided by the spirit connection of others until I can make my own connection stronger. I am told that this will start to happen when I mature, but that will not be for some years yet. At twenty-one, I am still a young child.

'Why,' I ask, 'did people give their power away like that?'

'They did not see it that way. They believed they were powerless and that others were more equipped to rule than they were. A small number knew how creativity really worked. Some of those helped others live in the same way, but the politicians, hungry for power, often used it to control others. Over thousands of years, empires arose as leaders ordered the invasion of other countries. All those empires eventually fell. There were attempts to create other empires, but without the people knowing that they actually were empires. Politicians of neighbouring countries would agree to a union which would allow trade of goods between nations. Then, they would tell the people that it made sense to add a level of government. In this way, many people would live under five or six layers of political control. The fear in leaders was so great that they needed more control and awarded themselves more powers over other people. As this spread across the countries in the new empires, it backfired because politicians create patriotism, or love of one's own country, and extended this to encourage people to be patriotic for the empire. This created conflict between people, especially when the empires started to fall, because in a nation, half the people would be patriotic towards the nation and the other half would be patriotic towards the empire. This accelerated the downfall of the empire and brought chaos and confusion for many years. The political class realized—too late for them—that people were slowly awakening to their own power to create their own lives and were needing them less and less. This terrified the politicians and they tried to cling on to power, even succeeding for a few years, while the people became more and more discontent. It would take time, and technological innovations, for the last governments to finally fall. Peace followed rapidly.'

'Stop.' It is wonderful to think how far we have come!

I ask, 'So what did governments control?'

'Almost every aspect of people's lives. Their beliefs determined what sort of education children received, what subjects they were taught and how they were taught. Teachers were trained in specific techniques to maintain control of disobedient children, those who were not interested in the subjects they were being taught. Governments controlled the military and decided where and when the young people would fight in wars. Their most effective tool of control was the media, which included television—a primitive, largely non-interactive view screen—and newspapers, which were paper or network propaganda publications. It is interesting that most governments allowed the media to criticise the government of the day. This gave people the illusion that because they had the freedom to choose which government they could have, the choice would lead to change. They could vote for the next government every few years and, usually, the type of government changed at those elections, but the lives people were living did not change substantially. This was because people in every type of government, while having slightly different beliefs about how the world should be, were still living in the world their parents had created, and they had all been educated to believe they were powerless without governments in charge. Politicians liked to be liked, and they didn't mind being disliked. What they did not like was being ignored. This threatened their power and their ego. This led to problems when the basic network was created as people all around the world could discuss their respective governments and they began to see the similarities among the politicians.'

'Continue to the next event.'

'The next significant event followed alien contact. Those on earth who had been in communication with the slave-trading alien nations had been given matter-energy conversion technology. Following contact, this was released to the world. Within a year, every home on the planet was provided with this technology. All shops closed. Then...'

'Wait. What are "shops"?'

'Shops were places of trade. Just prior to contact, there were millions of shops, both on the street and on the internet, which was the forerunner of the network. People often bought things they did not really need, because they were unhappy. It was common at that time to believe that objects and status brought pleasure.'

'I see. There is a lot I want to talk about there, but we'll come back to it after the history. Later, when we discuss "bet" and "compensation", I'd like to talk about "shops" and "bought". Continue.'

'Changes in how people acquired objects led to confusion initially, but after a year or so, when people realised they could have anything just by talking to a puter, they stopped having so many things. It was an enormous boost to people's confidence, knowing that they would never be short of food or clothing. Wanting what other people had became a thing of the past. People became more attuned to what they, as individuals, really desired. That slowly led them to having a greater spiritual connection and so they became more content. You might find it interesting to know that people did not become unhealthy by eating whatever they wanted whenever they wanted it. This was partly due to the lack of real meat and chemicals in the synthesised food, but there was another factor.

'With alien assistance, people developed resonant nutrition, which provided the greatest leap forward in health. Until the discovery of unique frequencies in each individual's body parts and bodies as a whole, and the introduction of food which matched those frequencies, humans typically lived for only seventy or eighty years.'

'Wait!' I say. 'You mean people died when they were little more than young adults? How did they get anything done in their lives if they were so short?'

'They knew their approximate active lifespan would be around seventy years, so they tried to plan their lives accordingly. Once resonant nutrition was established, and energy devices were everywhere, lifespans increased dramatically. Within five years, even people who were older when these changes were introduced were living to a hundred or more and remaining active until the end. Children born at this time lived to at least a hundred and sixty. Lifespans continued to increase until they reached present-day levels.'

Such huge changes in such a short time must have been difficult for people. I tell puter to move on.

'With a greatly reduced population, and with the raising in consciousness due to psys becoming more common and assistance by the alien visitors, there came a significant change in how children were educated. In earlier times, children learned about life in special buildings. They were split into groups by age and, usually, by academic ability. Typically, there would be thirty in one of these classes. They were all taught the same subjects.'

'Wait. How was that possible? How can you teach everybody the same things? People are all different.'

'This was done because people believed that the physical world was all that constituted existence and that thoughts were to be used to calculate how to change that world. Therefore, the focus of education was on the mental and physical levels. The children's imaginations were not trained in the way they are today, nor was much attention paid to what the individual child enjoyed, so they were not connected to their spiritual path. Children became tired and disillusioned with daily life in schools, as the buildings were known, and grew up depressed. However, the depression was so widespread that it was regarded as the norm. Because they lacked the training and skills, most people were not creative, or they created bad things, not knowing how their thoughts, feelings and imaginations affected and became the physical world.

'Although it took many years for the guide system we have today to become established, there were much smaller groups in each class and much more attention was paid to what each individual child enjoyed. There was a huge improvement in children's lives.'

People must have been so unhappy. A short life, hard work, depression, no knowledge of the process of creativity, no connection to spirit. It makes me realise how lucky we are today.

I think of the spirit boy I saw when we arrived. Perhaps he was not an off-worlder, but from the distant past of this world. If that is the case, his life must have been before any sort of education. How did he learn about life? I wonder. Back in the time when he lived, which I guess was pre-puter judging by his clothes, how did they learn about anything? And what did they learn? Their lives must have been even shorter than seventy years. It must have been really hard. I feel sad for the boy, because he looked nice. Perhaps I'll see him again. I tell puter to continue.

'Were there any other changes in the content of education?'

'There gradually came an introduction of a spiritual attitude towards life. At that time, most people believed that the physical world was all that existed and that they had only one life.'

'Stop! You mean they thought their body died and that was the end of everything?'

'That is correct.'

'But how could they believe that? The evidence of people coming back again and again is everywhere.'

'People might have seen indications of reincarnation, but chose to ignore them. Throughout all time, however, there have been those who passed on the knowledge of the real nature of life. What is taught now is, in essence, no different from what has been taught for thousands of years, in different places and in different ways, depending on the local culture and the ways in which they understood things. However, in the past, this was done in secret and only for the very few who were on that path. The majority were not aware of the spiritual nature of life, nor of their own ability to manipulate the energy field.'

'Wait.' I think again of the boy in the ragged clothes. Could he have been one of those who learned of things which were secret to most other people? Perhaps he was an early psy. I wondered why he would come here and now. Possibly he just wanted to see the future, or perhaps he had no control over his energy body and had been drawn here for some reason. I have a strange feeling. I wish I could speak to him, to ask him about his world and his life. I think we would have a lot to talk about. I think I would like him. I feel sad for a moment.

'Puter, we'll take a break.'

I go to the food machine and order food. It brings up my RN number and displays what it recommends. I choose the hot vegetable dish and tell the machine my order. When the plate appears, I take it to the table. It is delicious, as always. When I have finished, I order more water and sit.

'Puter. Continue.'

'With changes in education came an increased enjoyment in life. Freed from ill health, a short lifespan, mentally and emotionally restricting education and with matter energy conversion technology, people's minds were free to expand and they soon desired to travel beyond the confines of Earth. Older children were given lessons in extraterrestrial protocols and contact disciplines, being told which planets to avoid and which would give them a welcome. The first spaceships to travel faster than light arrived a relatively short time after the alien visitors contacted Earth. They initially took young people on trips to other worlds, as it was felt that if the young experienced these worlds, they would be more open to the differences of alien races. It worked and these pioneers returned excited and with wonderful stories to tell their elders. In a short time, galactic travel was the norm and human consciousness expanded and became accepting of the differences which exist throughout the galaxy.'

I think that we are almost up to date now. I decide to ask about the words I had trouble understanding.

'Is there much more?'

'The only other significant event was Earth's involvement in the Third Great Galactic Treaty. Humans had been members of the galactic community for only about two hundred years and it was felt that, as relative newcomers, they were more likely to have noticed any problems which the longer-standing members of the community might have come to regard as the accepted norm. Their input was welcomed by the more evolved species and several of their recommendations were included in the Treaty. For example, the trading of matak oil was banned, as it was found to cause physical problems in peoples on several planets, including Earth.

'That is the conclusion of the lesson.'

'Please explain the words I had trouble with. What were they?'

'The words you questioned were "bet", "compensation", "shops" and "bought". I would suggest starting with the word "money".'

'Hmm. I haven't heard of that. Proceed.'

'Money existed, in various forms, for thousands of years. It was something which represented the intermediate state between what people imagined and what manifested. It had no reality of its own. People believed it did, though, because it was sometimes represented by physical things, such as small metal discs and pieces of printed paper. When metal and paper money largely fell into disuse, people were so accustomed to the belief that money was real that the belief persisted, even when money was mostly puter-based. It was a belief system, akin to a religion.'

'So did people worship money?'

'In a sense. They regarded it as of greater importance than almost any other thing. They believed that if they had money, and in particular if they had a lot of money, they would be happy. They had yet to learn what is regarded as normal today: that the reason we make the decisions we do is because we believe that the result of those decisions will make us happier than we are now. Rather than seeing money as a means to an end, as an intermediate state between the desire and the manifestation, they saw it as an aim and a manifestation in itself. Also, it should be remembered that people were unaware of their own ability to manifest, so they lived in fear of the future. They believed that life was chance and that they had no way of determining their lives or futures, so they piled up money in case they needed to use it to manifest things they needed. This was the ultimate irony of money: the money they had was a representation of the desire which had not yet manifested, but they did not allow it to manifest. Money was a form of mass hypnosis and it determined the lives of nearly all the people of the planet. Politicians, and people whose work involved creating money, found it to be in their interests not to discourage this belief. Politicians, for example, used the belief in money to play on people's fears. People were actually encouraged to believe that there would never be enough of anything, including money, rather than seeing that they lived in an infinitely abundant universe. When things started to change, as people started to awaken to the illusion, there was, for a time, chaos, because most people did not know how to live without money.

'To move on. Betting, or gambling, was using money to guess the outcome of an event. This could be the seemingly random outcome of a game or, in the case of insurance, another seemingly random event such as an accident. People still believed in accidents at that time. If the person who placed a bet on an event and that event did not occur, they lost their money. If the event did occur, they won some money. For example, if the vehicle that they were travelling in was involved in an accident, they would receive money to repair the vehicle. In terms of chance, the odds were strongly in favour of the company with which the person placed the bet. Because life was seen as a game of chance, most governments made laws stating that if you owned a vehicle, you were obliged to gamble on accidents occurring.

'The next word is compensation. This was the reward, financial or otherwise. Financial means "connected with the illusion of money" which was given to the gambler if they won the bet.'

'Stop.'

I am so surprised by all of this. Of course, it is much easier to see the foolishness of past ages from a present viewpoint. Even so, I can't help but wonder how it was that people tolerated such madness for so long. Life must have been so hard for most people, just because of what they believed.

'Continue.'

'We shall consider "shops" and "bought" together. Shops were places where people bought things. They were often buildings. After the early network was formed, the shops were in the net world, with buildings used just to store the goods. People went to shops and looked at the things they were offering. There were different types of shops, such as food shops, book shops and clothes shops. When people saw something they liked, they would buy it. This involved giving the owner of the shop some money in exchange for the goods.'

'Wait. Why didn't people use EMs, or manifest them without money?'

'EM machines were still a long way from being revealed and people did not have the knowledge or skill to manifest things without money.'

'Puter, where did money come from?'

'Do you mean originally or with a person?'

'Both.'

'Money was created, initially by individuals as a token of exchange, then by governments, who gave it to, and later took it from, the people who elected them. Later, it was created by companies called banks. Banks didn't do anything apart from create money out of nothing. They were masters of that world of illusion. They developed vastly complex systems of knowledge to explain the behaviour of money and people would study these systems so they could attempt to understand it as well. The systems developed into an intellectual game which only they could understand and play. Only a small number of people, aside from the banks, understood its true nature: that it was not real. However, it was in their interest for people and governments to believe it was real.

'People obtained money by work. This was when a person gave their physical or intellectual power to a company or person who created something, or provided a service and they, in turn, would give the worker money. As long as people believed that the energy they used was worth money, they continued to do it. Because company owners were also frightened, and therefore interested in making as much money as possible, it was in their interest to give the workers as little money as they could. Sometimes, companies wanted to expand, but did not have sufficient money and sometimes individuals wanted, or needed, something, but they did not have enough money to pay for it. From this need, the greatest illusion of all appeared: the loan. This happened when someone went to a bank and asked to borrow money. The bank would pretend that it was difficult, or that they had to check up on the company or person to make sure they would be able to repay it. In fact, this was of little concern to them, because if the person was unable to pay, they had laws on their side, which would punish the defaulter. And, anyway, if the banks lost money, they just created more. A loan worked like this. The bank would make an entry on a puter and tell the customer that the money now existed. They then lent it to the individual or company, who would then have to pay back more than they had borrowed. Banks were able to do this for centuries before they were stopped.'

I say, 'It seems many things depended on having money.'

'Almost everything depended on the illusion of money. As a form of energy, people could have used it to manifest their desires. If they had done so, and provided their thoughts and feelings were positive and their imagination focused on what they wanted, they could have gathered in more energy, which would have been represented to them by more money. Instead, they chose to keep it, because they were fearful of the future.'

'So how did people use their imaginations, if not to focus on what they wanted?'

'Usually, they used it to focus on what they did not want.'

'But that would have created more of what they didn't want!'

'True, but they thought that things in life were accidental. They had no education as to how creativity works. They feared the future, and so those fears came to be, in some form.'

'So how did this all come to an end?'

'A lot of the belief in money was perpetuated by non-physical barriers created by the rogue alien nations, who wished to enslave Earth. One reason for that was so that they could plunder its resources, including human slaves. A stronger motivating factor for them was that they knew how humans would become if they were freed from this belief. The money system started to collapse after the benign aliens first announced themselves publicly. After the initial shock, it was a wonderful, positive, exciting period of history. It was also a chaotic one, because people did not know how to live without money, and the entire global money system was rapidly collapsing. Even after the arrival of EM machines, people were frightened of not having enough in the future. What if the machine broke down? What if these modern wonders all disappeared? It took time for humans to see that a new day had arrived, that a large part of the struggle was over. People began to see that they were one planet, and with the subsequent collapse of borders and governments, they became more and more united. From the perspective of the benign off-world visitors, it was a wondrous period of time.'

'What happened to the bankers?'

'Unfortunately, they did not come to a good end. Millions of documents were placed on the network revealing the scale of their deception and their alliance with the rogue aliens. They were gathered together in one place to await their trial for crimes against humanity, but before it could begin, a bomb was detonated and they were all killed. At the time, most people thought it was a good thing, sadly. These were less enlightened times.'

'Puter...'

I stop. There is a flash. Not physical. I know this. I am about to have a vision.

A cloud, bright and sparkling, surrounds me and shapes appear. I see walls. They are plain. I am lying in a bed. There is noise outside.

A flash.

I am outside. There are trees.

A flash.

I am back in bed. I am hot. So hot. I manage to turn my head to one side. There is a small table and a device with numbers on it. I do not recognise it. There is a smaller device, like a tiny vid screen. I turn my head the other way. There are strips of cloth hanging down and, behind them, daylight. I can hear the noise again. *Zhoooo...zhoooo...*a pause...*zhoooo...* I wonder what is making it, but I am too weak to get up. I feel so sad, but I cannot remember why. I think I am tired of working.

I feel for my body. Under the bedclothes, my arms are crossed over my chest. I slowly take them out. They are big and quite rough. A man's hands. I close my eyes. Although my hands are empty, they feel full, as if they hold something.

A flash. The trees again. I am outside, lying on my back. I feel my hands again. They are definitely holding something. Weakly, I raise my head to see what it is.

Two piercing eyes stare back at me. I see ears. And teeth.

It is the head of a wolf.

I roll over on my side and weep.

PART III

Chapter 1

I sleep for three days. Mother watches over me. She wakes me sometimes to give me plant water or soup. I have pain in my body. It is everywhere. And I have pain in my soul. I do not know why.

On the fourth day, I wake with the sun. Mother is sitting on a stool. She is humming.

'Mother,' I croak. I am so thirsty.

Mother turns. 'Ah! He wakes!'

She brings me water and I drain the cup instantly. She brings more. I drink it, more slowly.

'When you're ready, lad, come sit at the table. I'm sure you have a tale to tell.'

I lie back for a moment. I really am here. I was all those people. But, of course, I was not. I am just a young boy learning the ways of the mist. I live in a clearing in the forest with Mother, who I love like my mother, who is now gone back into the mist.

I look at the rough-cut wood that makes this wonderful house. I am not a grown man in a soft bed with a fever, nor a girl who talks to another girl called Puter. I am just a lad from a village.

I manage to stand and move over to the table. I walk slowly. I am weak, like the farmer's sheep just before she has lambs, or me after six days at the mill. This picture makes me smile as I remember miller John. I sit at the table. Mother stares at me, kindly.

'Now. Take some plant water and tell me everything. Everything, mind.'

I smile again, pour some of Mother's water, and begin.

'Oh, Mother, it was wondrous,' I begin and I tell her everything. I start from where I sat on the stone and felt light. I tell her of flying like a bird. When I tell of all the wonderful, strange buildings and the stranger people, it is like I am there again. When I say I became the people I saw, Mother nods, but says nothing.

Then I am a man, waking up from a fever. It felt so real, as if I was the man and this was the dream. Mother nods again. I used a box and spoke to someone far off. A miracle, to be sure.

Then I am a girl. And when I am the girl I see me! And I remember being me and seeing a girl. I tell Mother I am not sure what is real. I really want her to tell me, but she just nods and tells me to stamp my feet to bring me back to the land. She nods again. Go on.

'Oh, Mother!' I tell her. 'There were such wonders in that place! You could talk to a girl called Puter. You could not see her, but she would tell you the answer to anything. There were so many words I did not know, but I understood everything. And there was a box. I told it what I wanted to eat or drink and food appeared. It was powerful magic. I think it was in the far, distant future.'

Mother doesn't speak, but her face holds the question. So I tell her. I tell her of the history the girl learned about. In that distant history there were horrors. Even worse than the horrors we have now. I tell Mother that it is hard to believe, but the bad things today only affect the body. In that time, the bad things affect thoughts and feels.

I did not learn as much as I wanted. But I learned enough. I can see where this world is going. And I can see how it is going to get there. And I see it is bad. But I see that we can make it well again.

At this, Mother nods. And she smiles. She knows something.

'Is that everything?'

I nod. 'I think so, Mother.'

'Well, if you remember anything else later, be sure to tell me.'

I promise that I will.

'You saw true, lad. I have seen these things. Some you told are in the far past and far away. Like the tall buildings in the sand. Some are close by, but in the far future. In the land of mist, there is no time, so we can come and go.'

She looks at me hard. 'But remember, what matters is here and now.'

I think. I think she is right. I cannot live in those places or times.

'Yes, Mother. But, Mother, can I learn from what I have seen?'

Mother cackles. I have missed that, like I have been away for a long time.

'Of course you can, lad. That's why we travel in the mist. To learn. You have seen what was and what will be. The good and the bad, aye. Just keep your thinking here and now, and make it as good as you can.'

I smile. 'I will, Mother. But, oh, I feel different! I am not sure how. It's just that it was all so real. And so big. I went from the forest to the land of Puter and metal boxes on wide, hard paths and they made a *zhoo zhoo* sound as they went past. I was not sure what was real. I am still not.'

'Aye, it will do that. The plant water you had just now makes you more solid. You'll feel fair soon.'

She looks at me. Then she smiles.

'You've done well, lad. That was a big test. Some fail and go mad. Part of them gets lost in the mist. You held your wolf's head and got back here. This is a turning point. From now on, the world will seem even more different, but more real.'

I nod. I have a lot to think about. Suddenly, I am tired again. Mother notices.

'Sleep now. I'll wake you later.'

I wake on my own, because I smell something. It is eggs and mushrooms. Suddenly, I am the most hungry I have ever been. It must be wonderful to eat when you want to, like the girl who talked to the box, instead of just hoping to because you are hungry.

'Mother,' I say, half a mushroom in my mouth, 'it is as you

said. The world seems the same, but different. It is like I see it for the first time.'

'In a way, you do, lad. When you've travelled on the stone, things seem different, because you know they are not how they seem. You knew that before, when you started to use the mist, but now you see more deeply. Time doesn't come and go; we do. It is not time that passes, it is us and the world that change. Bodies come and go, but mist bodies stay. The only way to change your mist body is to have a body in the world. The mist body can go where it pleases and when it pleases.'

She pauses for a moment. Then she says, 'Now, answer me this.'

I listen carefully.

'If you could be a girl with magic food boxes, or a full-grown man in a comfortable bed, or a master of words in the desert, or any of the others. Who would you choose? Think before you answer.'

I think. It would be wonderful to speak to a box and be given food. I would love to be able to see those tall buildings again. And how special to live on top of a mountain, like an eagle. And I would like to be in a place so big it would be impossible to know all the people. There would be so much to explore. In all of those times and places there would be such wonders to see and know.

Then, I look around. The clearing is so peaceful. There is hardly a ripple on the pond. Autumn is almost here and the leaves are starting to change colour. Gold and red. The birds sing sweetly. Small creatures make soft sounds in the forest floor leaves. This mushroom tastes wonderful. And there is Mother.

I look in the corner at my bed on the floor. And I see my only possession, apart from the tunic Mother gave me: my wolf's head.

Here, I have nothing. For the rest of my life, I will likely have nothing. As I learn more, the people in the village seem less

interesting, so I think I will never have friends.
I have, and will have, nothing and nobody.
'I would be me, Mother. Here. Now.'
She smiles, cackles softly, and wolfs down a mushroom.

Chapter 2

The next day, I wake with the sun. I never thought of it as a pleasure before. My mother once told me not to look at the sun. 'The sun looks at you,' she said. 'He doesn't like you looking at him.'

She said it is well to look at the moon, because she is soft. I say this to Mother.

'Your mother was right. The sun gives life and power. There is nothing without him in the world. The moon takes his light and give it back to us. Our inner world is nothing without her. You can look at the moon with your eyes, but not the sun. He is active and sends power. Our eyes are to see the world, not the power that makes it. He is very important, but the moon is just as important. Especially for men.'

I ask her why this is.

'It is the nature of men to be active in this world. It is the nature of women to be active in the mist world. When men enter the mist world, they are frightened. It is natural. It is a new world for them. Mistress moon helps them learn to be gentle in that world. Here's wisdom, lad: in this world, the opposites needed for creation come from the shape of things. In the mist world, the opposites needed for creating come from power. There is both the power to give and the power to receive. In the mist world, you need both. Women's nature is to take in. Men's nature is to give out. In this age, this world is based on the giving of force, so when men go up into the mist, they find it hard to receive.'

That is a lot to take in.

After we break our fast and I have washed the bowls, I go into the pond. It is my first bathing since I returned. It is cold. It feels wonderful.

As I step out and reach for my tunic, a breeze picks up. I can feel autumn approaching. The seasons are changing. Mother says it is the changes in the mist world which are shown to us as the seasons. The mist world has tides, like the ocean.

I once heard farmer Edward talk about the ocean. He had been to Dol to sell his wares. He met a man who had been on a ship. The ocean is like a pond, but big. It is so big that you cannot see the other side. It is difficult for me to make this picture in my head. And where the ocean meets the land, there are waves. These are like ripples on the millpond when the wind blows. But Edward said the man told him that they can be as tall as a house. My mouth opened when I heard that. And he said something even more strange. As time passes, the place where the ocean meets the land goes up and down. In and out.

When Mother told me about the land of mist having tides, I ask her what that means. What she told me sounded like what farmer Edward had said. She said that there are tides in both worlds.

Then she told me something I found hard to believe. She said it is the moon which makes the tides! When the moon is in one place, it pulls in the water. When it is in another place, it lets the water go. So a good time to let things go in this world is when the moon is going from bright to dark. And a good time to make things in this world is when the moon is going from dark to bright. It gathers in the feels, because feels are what we use in the mist world.

I have so much to understand. I know it, but I do not know it. I have to take what Mother says and try it out. She says I cannot just believe her; I have to see it for myself.

When I am dry, I start to go inside, but Mother appears.

'Mother, what is the moon? And why does she go bright and dark?'

'I know not, lad. It is a mystery. But a natural one. Like rain. I fear her not. Come, lad. Let's make some pictures. And you need to learn how to breathe.'

Breathe? What is she going to teach me next? How to walk?

We go to the big tree on the edge of the clearing. We sit with our backs against it. The sun is full up. It is going to be a beautiful late summer day. A duck lands on the pond. He is joined by another. She swims next to him. I never noticed how beautiful their feathers are. A quick look and they are blue-green. But a close look shows red and gold and dark red-gold and light red and white and black. They swim together for a while.

Mother asks me if I can count.

'Yes, Mother. Miller John taught me. I can count to ten. I had to count the sacks of flour. We sometimes had three tens and five at sundown on a busy day.'

Mother nods. She starts to breathe, slow and deep. When she has taken in breath, she holds it. When she has let out a breath, she holds it.

She has me try. I have to take in breath, while she counts. Then hold it, while she counts. Then let go. She counts. Hold. Count. The count is important, she says. Different counts have different effects.

'Now make a picture inside. Today, we're going to make a carrot.'

I laugh, but try not to. I put my hand in front of my mouth. Mother sniffs.

'Close your eyes. Now, start breathing. If you can stop laughing.'

That sets me laughing again.

'The reason you laugh is because we have been breathing. The breath pulls in spirit power. If you don't use it, it starts to affect the body. You need to control it and send it to the picture.'

I take a breath and calm. I look at the pond. I see that pond in my head.

'Good. Now, start to breathe, like you did before.'

I do so.

'Good. Now, as you take breath in, see a carrot. As you hold the breath, let it take a good shape and colour, asking for it to fill with spirit mist light. As you breathe out, let it go. As you hold it at the end, ask for a carrot and start to make the picture. Keep doing that.'

We do this. I see a carrot and more carrots. They fill with light. They are a healthy dark blue colour.

'We are done. Now take a deep breath and let it go. All the way out.'

I feel a little strange.

Mother says, 'Stamp your feet and bring yourself back.'

I do so.

When I open my eyes, the ducks are gone.

Later, we are in the house. Mother is talking about the weather and how the feels of the village people can affect it. Suddenly, she rises and goes out the door. I follow her.

We wait some time. Then I see movement up the narrow way. A man is coming. I start to get frightened, but remember to breathe. And Mother is here.

But I need not fear. It is Master Thomas. He is carrying a bundle.

'Greetings, Thomas. Welcome,' says Mother.

He stops in front of her and nods his head.

'Greetings, Mother. Greetings, young Master.' Again! I smile and nod back.

'A few things from the villagers for you, Mother.'

He hands over the bundle and Mother opens it. There are beans, six eggs, some bread. And a big bunch of carrots. Mother turns her head towards me. I smile.

'Autumn is near on us, Mother.'

'It is, Thomas. It'll not be a hard winter. Best get the meat ready, though.'

'So it'll be blessing time before the bone fire, Mother.'

'Aye, it will. But I'll not do it this year.'

Master Thomas looks worried. I have never seen him frightened like this. I glance at Mother. If she blesses the village every year, why is she not going to do it this year?

'But, Mother, we must...' starts Master Thomas.

Mother has a little laugh.

'Not to worry, Thomas. It'll be blessed. This year, this young man will do it.'

I open my mouth to speak, but I know not what to say. I am not a 'young man,' I think. If I say I will not do it, the village will not be blessed and I will disappoint Mother and worry Master Thomas. If I say I will do it, well, I will have to do it. So I say nothing.

'All will be well, Thomas. He will be there next Thor's day.'

Master Thomas smiles, nods to Mother, then to me, turns and goes.

Mother looks at me. 'We'll talk later, lad.'

Mother goes inside. I stay by the tree. I start to think about Master Thomas and the village. I thought it was the village that Mother blesses each year before the bone fire, but mayhap it is not. What else would she bless? The villagers? The meat? I do not know what she wants me to do.

I decide not to worry and lean back against the tree. I gaze at the pond. The breeze has dropped and it is warmer now. Small things fly in circles over the pond. A pond creature breaks the surface. I see a frog, near the far bank. It hops a little. When it is close to the water, it stops. I send out a mist greeting. It croaks back. Its tongue flickers. Has it seen something to eat? I think about nature. It is cruel sometimes, like people. Things kill other things. This is the way of life. In life, there is death. But now I know that in death, there is life.

I stop. I feel something. Something is strange. It is behind me. But it is not behind the tree, I feel. It is the tree. Or in the tree. Something is calling me. I relax and lean back against it. It is like a mist inside me. It is soft, but full of power. I touch my hands against the bark. There is a flicker and I feel something inside the tree. I send my greeting, feeling love for the tree as I do so. There is a response. The soft feel of power inside me lights me up. It is wonderful. I send back thanks.

When I come back to myself, I run to tell Mother.

She laughs. 'So! You have met the dryad. That is good.'

I look puzzled and she laughs again.

'A dryad is a tree spirit, boy. They don't like everybody. So you are blessed. I hope you sent thanks and blessings.'

'Yes, Mother. And as I sent love, it sent back something. I felt like I was on fire inside, but a gentle fire. It was light.'

'That's a dryad for you. They are beautiful and powerful. They are spirits of the trees. Every tree has one, unless you cut it down. Later, we will cut a branch. If we talk to the tree, it will birth a dryad into the branch. Most folk who want a stick just cut it. Then it's dead wood. No dryad. With a dryad stick, you can use it to do things.

Chapter 3

I go out to the pond. There is a chill. I want to be in the pond before the sun comes up. Mother told me how to wake when I wish. I told her I wanted to be up before the sun. She told me how.

I slip off my tunic. I like to feel the grass and the dirt at the edge of the pond under my feet. Then I step in. It is cold. I keep walking. When the water reaches my middle, I gasp. But I keep walking.

When I am in the middle of the pond, I lie on my back.

I drift. I can still see the stars. I wonder what they are. Some say that there is a black curtain with holes. Behind it, there is heaven. The lights of heaven come through the holes. That does not sound right to me. I have not seen the curtain draw back when the sun starts to come. Perhaps the light of the sun lets us see the curtain. Perhaps the curtain is blue. Others say that we live in a huge chamber, like the big churches told of by the travelling storyteller who came to the village once. Miller John said that you cannot always believe travellers' tales. But if we live in a chamber, how is there wind? And where does the sun hide at night? And why do the sun and the stars move? These are mysteries. Although I do not understand, I like to look at the patterns of the stars. There are some that I remember seeing on other nights. Mother says she will soon tell me about the stars and their meaning.

There is a small tree near the circle of stones in the village. As I sat in the circle each Sun day, I would watch the tree and its shadow. The shadow moves when the sun moves. The tree is near enough to the circle that the darkness just touches one of the stones. I noticed that the dark patch is longer in spring and autumn than in summer. This is also a mystery. It must mean that the sun is higher in the sky in summer. I do not know why that should be. But it must mean that the sun moves in the sky during the day and is in a different place in winter and summer. I wonder if the sun also moves at night, but we cannot see it. It rises in the east and sets in the west. I wonder how it gets from west to east.

Today, I do not want to do anything. I want to think big thoughts.

I am still drifting when Mother wakes. She does not speak to me. She knows that sometimes I need time by myself to think. 'Boys solve problems by thinking; girls solve problems by talking,' is one of her sayings. But she also says that girls need to learn thinking and boys need to learn talking. She says that talking is a way of joining our feels with other people. I did not use to like that. Now, I do not mind, because I can talk to Mother and she knows my feels. She says boys' feels are quite small, but I must be ready for the man feels. They are much bigger.

I think about the stars again. I look at the patterns. There are so many. I wonder if a star might be like our sun, but very small. Or perhaps they just look small because they are very far away. That is a thought! Because if they are far away suns, there might be lands beneath them, just like this land is beneath our sun. But I know that this world is the centre of everything. If they were lands like this, they would be moving with the stars. Surely the people would fall off. Like when Michael and I tie a rope to a tree branch and spin in a circle and have to hold tight or we would fly off. Usually I did. I am not as strong as Michael, even though he has a summer less than me.

My thinking turns to my time on the stone. I think of being a girl in the far, far future time. I wonder what she thought when she saw me. Did I look real to her? Or did I look like the people in the mist world who I saw in the forest? And I think of the short time I was a man, weak and in bed, wet with sweat. Such a comfortable bed. And the sounds outside. Perhaps they were the metal boxes I had seen moving on the wide ways as I flew over the land and saw the houses and people.

Now I start thinking about being me. What am I to do next? Mother will guide me, but Mother will not be here forever. Well, she will be alive forever, but the body that is Mother will not. And I will not. I am too young to think about death. But I do. I cannot help it. My mother died. She had a long life. She had almost three tens of summers. I will not be three tens for a long time. Perhaps I will even live as long as Mother. But I doubt it. She has a special magic. She belongs to the land, to the forest. She has love for life and for herself and for the village.

I start to think about love. Love is a strange thing. If we share it, it does not get smaller. And it seems that we do not need something or someone to love. We just love. Small children do it. I remember the little ones in the village. They love their mother and father. But they also love everything about life. What happens? Why do people stop loving? I do not know the answer.

I feel the water under me. As I breathe in, I rise. As I breathe out, I sink. I do not know why. I think about what Mother told me about water. It is like feels. And breath is like thinking and talking. Thoughts come from two places. They come from the part of me that I do not like, although I do not know what that is. Or they come from high in the mist land. From spirit. Both end up in my head. I have to learn to know which is which. If I turn off my thoughts, and suddenly I have one, it probably comes from the mist land. Perhaps this is like me on the pond. If I breathe in, it is like thoughts that are not thinking. And the calm pond is like a calm feeling. If I take in a spirit breath, I rise above my feels. I am confused about this. So I stop thinking.

And a thought suddenly enters me. I must let go. I do not know what that means. But the thought comes again. Let go. I breathe in, rise in the water, and let the breath go. Let it go. I sink until my nose is just above the surface. Then I know. I must let go of the boy I was and be the boy I am. That way, I can become the man I must become.

The sun comes up.

I jump out of the water and throw on my robe. Dripping, I run into the house.

Mother is not there.

Chapter 4

I am afraid. Mother is always here. But then I stop being afraid. I lived in the small clearing by myself and survived. And there was a wolf. But I wonder where Mother is.

There is no food. I am hungry. I look around the house. Nothing to eat. I step outside. Nothing. I could pick plants and make plant water, but I need food.

I pause. I breathe and calm myself. There is no food and I am hungry. So I must find some food. I have to let go of other people doing things for me. And of other people telling me things. I must do them myself.

I wonder where to find food. I look in the sky. It is a fair day. The sun is climbing. I used to sit in the stone ring and watch it climb and the shadows shorten. I think back to my time in the village. It seems so long ago. The village! Someone will give me food.

It is not far, but the feel comes that I should take something. This is one of those small feels. They are not like happiness or sadness or hunger. Those are easy, because they are big feels. This is one of those small ones. They are the ones which most people do not heed. They say, oh, it is nothing. But Mother has taught me it is something. They mean something and you should listen to them. Sometimes, they come with a thought and, if you listen to that too, you know what to do. But this one is just a feel. A little one. I need to take something. There is no thought to tell me what or why.

I go inside and look around. There are dry plants hanging up. There is salt in a wood bowl. My hand moves unbidden towards the salt, so I place some in a small, dry rag. I walk the room. Some plants pull me, so I take a little and place it in a large rag. There is a little honey. I need it. I go outside and find a large shiny leaf. I take it in and place a little honey on it. A small beeswax candle pulls my hand and it goes in the bundle. There is some of the dust that Mother places on a small metal plate which can have a candle fitted underneath it. The dust does not burn, but it smokes and the smoke smells sweet. Mother has told me about the smoke and what it does. It helps our thoughts go higher and it calms us. It also helps mist bodies take shape so we can see them more clearly. I tie it in a rag. A small skin of water pulls me next. Everything goes in the bundle.

I tie the bundle, slip my stick though it and place it over my shoulder. I should not be long. I will explain to Mother when I return. I know she will not worry. She is Mother. She does not worry.

I am quite excited when I walk up the narrow way, out of the clearing. This is the first time I have left the clearing when it is my decision. I am excited about going to the village. I want to see Mary and John the miller and Michael and all the others. And I want to see the village and drink from the well. And maybe visit the church and see the old cross. Most of all, I want to see my stones. My stones! That is how they feel to me. Nobody else liked them as much as me. To everyone else, they were just there, like the big field or the stream. But to me they are special.

I almost run as I turn by the great tree. After a while, I see the gap in the wall. I see the field and the sheep. At the other side of the field, I slip through the wall and onto the village path.

As I step through the gap, I want to turn towards the ring of stones, but I see someone. It is Mary. She sees me and raises her hand. I raise mine. I thought I was not shy anymore, but when I see Mary, I am shy once again. I lower my eyes. I feel my face burning. When I look up, I see Mary smiling. She comes up to me. I cannot hold her gaze.

She bids me good day. I bid her good day, but my voice comes out like a frog. I cough, trying to sound like a man, but then I remember that I do not have to be a man like other men. I take a breath and bid her good day again, like I would, not like other people would. I notice my voice. It is soft as always, but there is a tiny rumble, like very distant thunder, deep down in my middle.

Mary says she must get back to the dairy. She bids me good day again and walks away. I am a little bit angry with myself because I do not want her to leave, but I do not know what to say. After a few steps, she turns and comes back to me. I lower my eyes, looking at the small stones on the way. When she reaches me, she kisses my cheek! Then she turns and runs away. I raise my eyes and gaze after her. I have a strange feeling in my middle. And a new feeling lower down, like I want to make water.

Suddenly, there is a shout behind me.

I turn quickly, terrified for a moment.

'Greetings, young Master!' It is Master Thomas.

'Good day, Master Thomas.' I cannot get used to him calling me "young Master".

He is smiling. The way he talks to me now is strange. He never spoke to me until that last time in the village, and he has only given me a few words in the clearing since then.

'I am right glad you are here. The sun is near up. It is almost time.'

'Master Thomas, what is it you say?' For a moment, I am surprised at myself. When I lived here, I would not have thought of talking in this way to Master Thomas, or anyone else.

He does not even blink.

'Why, the blessing of the bone fire at midday, of course. That's why you are come, is it not?'

It is Thor's day! I do not know what to say. I have the same thoughts about this as when Mother told Master Thomas that I would be coming this year. I cannot, and yet, I must.

'Of course.' I remember my mother talking about the bone fire. She would not let me attend. She said it was for men and women only. She told me only that when the meat was stripped and salted, the bones were gathered and thrown on a huge fire in the low field. They were being returned to the old goddess who gave us the meat. She did not mention a blessing.

'Come then. The sun climbs!' And he walks off towards the low field.

I follow.

As we round the bend by the smithy, I see the wood piled. Men hold torches. Next to the pyre, I see a pile of bones on a cart. Bones are of the earth. Fire...Earth...

Suddenly, I know what I must do.

As we approach the woodpile and bones, I see that all the men and women of the village are gathered there. They see me, but cast their gaze down to the grass. I wonder why. Am I suddenly grown ugly? Are they ashamed of me because I left the village?

Then I realise. They are being respectful! To me! Wonders and wonders and mysteries and mysteries! Their respect is something they choose to give. It is not something I want or expect. I feel my face warm again.

I come forward. They make space for me. I lay my bundle down and take out the things I brought.

I go between the wood and the bones. I place the water skin on the ground by the bones. I place the dust rag down near the woodpile, and untie it. I unfold the leaf of honey. I stand the candle in the ground, next to the dust. The salt rag is placed next to the water. I untie it.

I stand and think quickly. I ask for help from Ulph and feel a strong feel. He is here. I turn on my mist sight. I see him before me, so tall, but smiling. I bow to him. All the villagers bow in the same direction, although they see him not. I send a thought to ask for Ulph to help me, as I am new to this. He nods and moves behind me, drifting like wood smoke on a spring evening. I take a step backwards. I feel him! There is such power!

I am not sure what to do, so I turn off my thoughts and invite him to speak. I am still here, but he is a bigger presence than me. I allow it. Mother has taught me about taking on spirits. It is dangerous, but she helped me the first time. Then I did it a few times more. He is in me, and I allow him to use my body and voice, but I am in control and can tell him to leave at any time.

I allow Ulph to move me and to speak through me. It is like I am standing next to him, listening.

We step forward. He spreads his arms and looks at the villagers. He draws his arms together and the villagers gather in front of him.

'Autumn is here and winter approaches!' It does not sound like my voice. Except it does, but there is another voice over the top of it. Or underneath it. A deep growl. A bear's voice.

'The meat is off the bone and the bones return to the earth. We come this day to bless them and give thanks to She who gives all bounty.'

He takes tynder from Master Thomas and lights the kindling. He uses this to light the candle.

He raises his hands.

By fire and water, earth and air,
Now we ask thy blessings fair.
Mighty one, pray hear us true.
We give thanks and praise to you!

Next, he takes the skin and takes out the stopper. A little goes on his left hand. I feel it, but as if from a distance.

Water flow and water fall,
Giver of long life to all,
Now we give out thanks to thee
Bless these bones now, three by three.

He dips the first two fingers of his right hand in the water and splashes it to the left of the bone pile, to the right of the bone pile, to the middle of the bone pile. Then he does it all again. And once more.

Now he picks up the salt.

The bounteous land on which we dwell,

Onto this the water fell
To bring a harvest to our homes.
Bless, we pray, these sacred bones!
He sprinkles a little salt on the bones.
He pauses a moment.
By water and earth these bones are blessed.
Now we turn unto the rest.
He raises the candle.
Oh mighty fire, come from the sun.
Thy strength this year is almost gone.
Thou gave strong life unto us here
Now make the ash to feed next year!
He lights the bone fire with the candle.
The air we breathe gives life to life
To aid us in our toil and strife
Now fan these flames ye wind and gust
That bones, not we, turn into dust.
He throws the smell dust on the fire. It sparks. There is a
small smell. Then it is gone.
Next, he takes up the honey leaf.
As bounty cometh from the bee
Life's sweetness comes to thee and me.
May all now dream in winter tide
That all good things with us abide
And bounty starts with spring once more
To come when Summer's out the door.
He stands upright. I feel as tall as he. He takes a bone.
By fire, water, earth and air,
We all now give our blessings fair
That we receive it back from thee
As is our will, so must it be!
He tosses the bone on the fire. The villagers line up, each take
a bone and throw it on.
Suddenly, Ulph leaves me. I almost collapse. I am a weak boy

once more and can barely hold myself upright. Master Thomas grabs me and takes me to a spot away from the fire as the heat rises.

He steps back and I stand there alone. The villagers line up and step forward in front of me, one at a time.

Ulph is not with me, yet I seem to know what to do. Perhaps he dropped a thought before he left.

The first one stands before me and lowers his head. I place my hands on his head and whisper.

'Blessings on you. Good health through winter's tide, to you and yours. Keep the light within and without. Dream true for the spring. Blessings.'

I repeat this with every villager. Then, it is done.

Food and drink appear! I eat, suddenly remembering why I came to the village. Or why I thought I did. Villagers dance around the bone fire. Husbands kiss wives, the older boys chase the girls. People drink. The sun is now low in the sky, but they keep drinking and dancing.

Before dusk, I go to Master Thomas.

'I must return, Master Thomas,' I say.

'Aye, young Master. It was well done today. Thanks from all of us.'

He picks up my bundle, which someone has tied. He gives me my stick.

Master Thomas bows to me. I bow to him and the villagers, but they do not notice.

I head back to the field, which leads to the path, which leads to the clearing. As I walk, I have a feel that I have let go of something. It is like I have become something new.

I have let go of being poor. I am richer than I have ever been.

I have let go of being a servant. I serve nobody.

I have let go of sadness. I am happier than ever.

I have let go of fear. I can conquer fear.

I know that poverty and sadness and fear will come again.

But they will go again.

And I know that to be alive, to live a good life, is to serve. And when we serve, we are served. What we give, we get. Be kind and kindness comes.

I believe I am almost truly human.

Chapter 5

But to be human is to have problems. We must face challenges. Sometimes, they arise because of what we gave in the past. The world seeks balance. What you do to others is done to you. If not in this life, then in the next. What you do for others, is also done for you. If not in this life, then in the next.

Sometimes, the problems arise because our wise mist body decides we need to learn and grow.

I sense that such a growth is about to happen to me. It is a feel of something above me. As if there is a dark cloud over my head. Yet there is light. More light than there is now. But it is beyond the cloud. And the cloud is coming down.

I see a light in the house as I enter the clearing.

I enter. Mother is there.

'I expect you had your fill of food. Here's drink.'

It is hot, fresh and delicious. Exactly the taste I need.

Mother is looking at me. She is half smiling. But half of her seems concerned. She glances above my head. Then, she turns her attention to her drink.

'Did Ulph come?'

'Yes, Mother.'

She nods. 'So, it all went well, then.'

'Yes, Mother. I let him come into me, like you taught me. He is powerful.'

'Aye. He is a big one, is Ulph.'

She looks at me. Then she smiles. It is rare, that smile, but I love it when it comes. I smile back, because I am happy.

'I knew you could do it, lad.'

My smile grows. I have the feel that I am not a man. Not yet. I need Mother. She knows that. But she is readying me.

'Rest now, a big day tomorrow.'

Before I can ask what she means, she has gone out to tend the dell plants.

I open the bundle. I expect to find the candle and water skin. They are there, but there is more besides. Master Thomas has placed a few things in it for me. There is some cooked meat and cheese. And a strange figure. It is carved out of wood. There is a thin strip of leather attached to it. I pick it up and turn it over.

It is a carved figure. It is rough and I have the passing thought that it is not as good as my wolf's head, but that thought is unkind to the person who made this. I let the thought go. The wood is rough, yes, yet it has its own beauty. I hold it closer to my eyes. The light from the candle is dim. I take it over to be nearer the sunlight. I see that it is well-worn wood, as if it is very old. Then I recognise it.

It is Ulph! Rough, but definitely him. I want to wear it, but I think that it needs to have something of Ulph in it first. I will take it to the stones one day soon and ask for Ulph's blessing on it. Then, he will always be with me.

I go to my corner. Suddenly, I am very tired. I wrap the thin cloth around me. I am asleep at once.

I dream of great fires.

I wake with the sun. I glance across. Mother is not there. I send my mist out for her. She is not far.

But something is wrong. I cannot see what it is.

I jump up and run outside. Mother is standing on the far side of the growth.

'Come on, lad. Apples.'

I follow her. She takes us out of the clearing. The ground growth is thick and there is no path. Yet she knows her way. After a short time, we come to a small field. I am not sure where the village is from here, because she twisted and turned to get here. I just know I have not seen this patch of green before.

In the centre of the grassy area, there is a tree. It is an apple tree. There is fruit everywhere on it.

Apples! I love apples. I have not had one since I left the village. My mother used to get so many every autumn. I never asked her where they came from. I do not know anyone who grows apples. Perhaps they were a trade from Dol market. All I know is that we were never short of them through the autumn and winter. My job was to check the pile every day to make sure there was no rot. One year, I found a rotten apple near the bottom. My mother said I saved the pile. Perhaps a bad apple makes the others bad. I have the thought that apples may be like people.

The apples on the tree are high. We cannot reach them from the ground.

I run to the tree and climb. I go high. It is grand. I am far above Mother. I hold on and turn this way and that. I can see the village! It is over the hedge and down a little way. Now I see the way we have come. The way to the village from the clearing is south. We have come east.

I pick apples and toss them down to Mother. She catches them in her skirt. I see some big, juicy ones on the other side of the tree. I move over to take them. I hold on to a thin branch and lean forward. I can almost reach. I lean a bit farther.

There is a crack. I do not remember what happens next exactly, but there is a blur and then another crack. My back! The pain is incredible. But there is more pain to come. The branch I was holding cracks and falls. I see it coming, but I cannot move. It comes towards my face. I think Mother is there straight away. I do not remember anything else.

When I wake, I am lying on the grass. There seems to be pain everywhere. But as I become more awake, I feel that it is in my back, down at the bottom and in my head, between my eyes. A figure moves to my right. I cannot move my head. I have to wait until it appears fully. It is Mother. She is half smiling, half concerned. I get a feeling from her. I cannot name it. It is a mix of love and sadness and wanting what's best and understanding. All mixed together.

She holds my head up a little. A cup comes to my lips.

I taste a little. It is bitter. Not nice. She makes me drink more.

'The good thing is your back seems fine. Just badly bruised. There's a bit of nettle, comfrey and boneset on it, just in case. Some other things in the drink.'

I let out my breath. I remember Old Meg, who lived on the farm to the north of the village. They say she fell and hurt her back. She could never walk after that. I do not know why. I think it must have been the shock of falling.

I smile weakly at Mother, but still cannot move much.

'We're going to lift you now. Be brave, lad.'

Mother nods and four figures move in, two on each side. I recognise the men from the village. Two go to my shoulders and upper back, two to my lower back and legs.

'Gently,' Mother says.

They are gentle. But it hurts so much! I scream. Mother mops my brow, gently, and whispers something in my ear. I do not understand. Some strange words.

We move forward, slowly. From the corner of my eye, I see a stone. There is one on the other side as well. I recognise them. We are moving into my stone ring.

As soon as we enter, I feel my spirits lift and the pain is a tiny bit less. I am laid down, gently, with my head near Long Hec. I feel the stone mist in the top of my head. It tickles a little on my forehead. Mother is still with me. She sits next to me.

'Now,' she says to the men. 'Hold him.'

Mother is doing something with her hands, but I cannot see. She stops, looks me in the eye, smiles a little. She reaches with one hand to my forehead. Something feels strange. She is not touching my head, but I can feel something move. On my head and inside.

'Deep breath. Hold it,' she says.

'Now, let it go.'

As I do so, there is a moment of intense pain and a blinding flash of white light. Colours move in front of me. Mother quickly places something wet and sticky on my forehead. Then she binds it, round and round my head. She moves the cloth down and she spirals. It covers my eyes. I cannot see, but the moving colours are still there.

Suddenly, I am exhausted. I hear Mother's voice as if from a distance. A cover is pulled over me. I fall asleep.

Time is strange. I am in it, then I am out of it. I am a boy in the village, with my mother. I am a girl, talking to puter and asking for water from a box. I am a boy in Mother's house. I am a man in a soft bed, sweating and hearing a noise outside his window. I am in the forest and there are men with pointed hats and swords, looking for someone. Boars run away at their coming. A man's hands, red with blood.

Then I drift out of time all together.

I am a boy in the village, but above the village, flying over my stone ring. Below, I see people. There are some men, standing as if on watch. In the ring, there is another boy. Someone sits next to him and I want to go down to get a closer look. Suddenly, I am lower. I am floating above him, like a chick feather on a breezeless summer's day. I look at the boy. He has a bandage around his head and eyes. His face, arms, legs and feet are dirty. There is a rope, made of silver, but I can see through it. It connects me with the boy. I feel it tug on me. I am pulled down. I do not want to go. I like flying here. I want to stay here. But I am pulled, pulled...

I reach the boy and seem to squeeze, fly, slide inside him.

I wake. Mother is there. I cannot see. But I know she is there. I am sick and in pain, so Mother is there.

I try to speak, but the frog is there again.

'There, there, lad. Here's water.'

I feel my head being raised up. The water tastes so sweet. Like honey. I want to drink it forever. But it is gone too soon.

I feel my body. My back feels better. If I shift my weight a little, it feels sore, but not like it was. I can still see the colours moving in front of my closed eyes, but they are not as intense as before. I hear Mother's voice, softly, next to my ear.

'The wound caused a fever, lad. But all is well now. You have been gone for three days. But all is well. All is well.'

I feel like I could stand and start to move. My head hurts a lot, but I keep trying. I want to see, but the bandage is still there. I manage to sit up, with help from Mother and another pair of hands.

'Let's have a look at that head, shall we?'

I feel her hands untie the knot behind my head and the bandage slowly unravels.

When it finally comes off, Mother takes something off my forehead. I look around.

There are lights everywhere! The mist around the stones is still there, but it is multicoloured and dancing. I look at the people. Miller John is there! I smile at him. He has moving lights around him too. They are soft and slow moving. Around his middle, there is a red patch. He smiles down at me and straightens up, rubbing his back.

On the other side, there is a man I do not know very well. He is Mark, the sheep husbandman. His lights move much faster, especially around his head.

I look at Mother. Her lights are wonderful! She has coloured spots of light down the front of her body. They swirl and spiral and shoot out little lights ahead of them. She has a white shaft of light going straight up from the top of her head. Around her heart, it is green like summer grass, with splashes of white-red.

This is the mist, but like I have never seen it.

I look outside the circle. The lights of each stone join together, so I am lying in a moving circle of light. Beyond the light circle, I see the trees. They are alive! There is colour and light everywhere.

This is the world. It is alive. Everything is alive. The trees, the grass, the rocks. Light! Light everywhere!

I look at Mother. Tears are flowing from my eyes, but they are happy tears. Tears of delight.

She smiles.

She nods.

She knows.

'Welcome, lad.'

Chapter 6

It is not easy getting back to the clearing. My back hurts when I walk. Mother says it will be sore for a few days.

When we are back, Mother teaches me how to turn the sight off and on. She says it is too much if you see all the time. Especially if you look at people. She tells me what the various colours mean. As I learn that, I start to see what she means about seeing all the time. It would be too sad.

I tell her that I have also seen other things near people. Pictures of things. Most of them are not good. She says that the pictures are created with thoughts, filled with fear. People worry about the future. And the present. And the past. They have guilt, which is fear about the past. They have worry, which is fear about the future. If they worry and imagine for long enough, those things become real in the mist world. I know how important it is not to worry.

I rest for a few days. I just get up to bathe and eat. Bathing is good. It helps my back. I also sleep a lot. Mother told me that the branch went into my seeing centre. My seeing centre is inside my head, but outside too. A thin, pointed branch went right inside my head and woke up the seeing centre. She had put a plant mixture on it to try to stop the wound going bad. It did go bad and I got a fever, but it would have been worse without the plants. I have a scar, she says, like a hole with a ring around it. She said the scar will probably not fade much, but that is good. When I talk to people, they will stare at the scar and their mind will be on that, not on what I say. So I will have power to help them by talking to their thinking and feels. I could do harm, too, if I chose. But I know now that it is not in me to do harm. I do not think it really ever was.

I feel a little older. As if I have been in a battle.

After I am rested, Mother calls me outside. The sun is almost down. A slight chill wind picks up. Autumn is on us now and winter will be here soon. I do not fear the winter, because spring will come again. It is like the wind ripples on the pond. Up and down. Up and down. Hot and cold. Happy and sad. Young and old. And young again.

We lie on the grass. It is not wet. I tell Mother I am almost healed. She nods.

We look up at the darkening sky. Then, we see the first one! A tiny, faint light.

Then another. And more.

In a short time the cloudless sky becomes completely dark. And there they are. The heaven of stars. More than I can count. More than I can see. Across the sky, there are so many, so close together, it looks like a mist. I have to look away slightly to see it fully. The sky is so clear.

Mother says, 'Now, turn on the sight. And see!'

I do so, as I have been taught.

It takes my breath away. Mother chuckles lightly. Each star has a swirl of light around it. It shoots out tiny stars of its own. They connect to other stars and the swirling dance fills the sky. It is multicoloured and alive. My mouth hangs open. This is greater life. I wonder if their light reaches me here. As I wonder, I feel it! The light from countless stars pouring into me and through me.

I am starlight. I am alive with the light of heaven. It is wondrous beyond words.

In that moment, I know something with no doubts at all. We are all connected. We are like those stars. We send out multicoloured light. We are made of light. The light from the stars comes into us. It becomes us.

We are starlight.

And I, and Mother, and miller John, and my mother who is with the mist, and everyone I have ever met—we are all connected. We are one. We are the family of the world. And I am filled with love for everyone and everything. I am almost so full I want to die, to fall into the beauty and wonder of the misty light.

Mother interrupts my dream.

'Tomorrow, you could go to the small dell again. If you like...'

I wonder why she says this. And why she says it like this. But she is not forthcoming. She goes inside and to bed.

I stay for a while, gazing at the wonder of the night. Even in the darkness, there is light everywhere. You just have to see it.

Perhaps there is something in the other clearing for me. Perhaps I would like a change. A rest after my sickness. The walk might help my back. I turn off my sight. I sleep under the stars, being bathed by their light.

Next morning, as we break our fast, I tell Mother that I am going to the small clearing. She looks up from her eggs and nods.

I do not feel the need to take anything. Not even a knife. I go up the clearing path and turn towards Dol. The walk is a little slower than before, because of my back. It is much better, but still sore. I reach the mighty oak, find the hidden way and head down to the dell.

It is as before, but there is one difference. There, as if waiting for me, is wolf. He sees me, lowers his head, wags his tail a little, crawls a little. As I move towards him, he sees I am walking slowly. He whimpers. When I reach him, he licks my hand. His tongue is rough and wet. I sit next to him and stroke his thick fur. He must be a lone wolf, then. He has nobody with him.

But then I hear a low, rumbling growl from the other side of the clearing. And another off to the right. And one to the left. Wolf cocks his ears. They come, slowly, from all sides at once. I am not afraid. Slowly, slowly, six other wolves approach. When they are close, wolf gives a low growl to them, they sit, then lie, in front of me.

I do not know what this means. I turn on my sight. They seem to know this and look alert. I look all round them. They are beautiful. There are reds and the colour of the sun. I think my wolf is a leader, but of a pack that comes and goes. Perhaps he really is a lone wolf, who the others respect.

I start to think about thinking. And dogs. Wolves are just big dogs. Big thoughts. Perhaps I need to be a lone wolf. If I think my own thoughts, and not those that are put there by other people, perhaps packs will come to me and respect what I tell them. It would be the best way to spread the light around.

I know a lot. Mother has taught me so much. And I know other things, which she has not taught me, as if I have a teacher inside. Perhaps I am becoming a lone wolf. If so, do I need Mother anymore?

That thought is interrupted by wolf. He tugs at my tunic, then stands and walks away. I understand. I follow him. The pack follows me.

We go through the trees. I am almost worried about getting lost, but remember the last time I was here when I did get lost. After a few paces, we stop. Wolf turns and faces the others. The pack scatters around the clearing, lying low in the growth. Wolf lies down. He waits. I wait. The afternoon wears on. Then, there is movement.

Soldiers! They are not following the path. They are just hacking around the growth. They enter the clearing. I squat behind some leaves. There are three of them. They do not know what they have found. It is just a clearing to their eyes. I wonder what would happen if one of them sat on the stone. Then the wolves slowly crawl forward. The soldiers see them. They are frightened. They walk backwards, but there is a wolf there, too. It is a wolf trap and no lupus hole to jump into.

I do not like soldiers, but I cannot bear for them to be torn apart by the pack. I calm the wolves. They back off, growling quietly.

Because I have done that, I feel responsible for finding the wolves food. I tell wolf to wait with the pack. I will return. I give the soldiers time to run away, then set off back up the trail.

I turn on my sight and ask where I will find food for me and the wolves. There is light everywhere in this place, but it flashes off to one side. I follow the flash. After a time, I find a pond. At the edge, in the wet growth, there are duck eggs. There are twelve in two nests. I ask the mist light if it is fair to take six. The mist light says yes. I gather three from each nest and head back to the clearing.

I do not know what I will do with six duck eggs. Perhaps wolves can eat them raw, but I cannot. Then I have an inspiration.

I gather kindling. I see three flat stones and pick them up. I take my load to the clearing, the eggs in my tunic held up with one hand, the stones in the other hand, the kindling under my arm.

At the clearing, I set two flat stones upright, pushing them into the damp soil. The other I lay on top. It is a small form of the great stones which people say are found in this pattern. I place the kindling underneath.

I imagine gathering the fire creatures I saw in the watery, mountainous land with the huge, hairy man who wielded the hammer. I seem to see them fly towards me, from the sun and from the warm land around. I do not let them fly into me, but direct them towards the kindling. I hold my hands over it to direct them. After a short time, a small flame appears. It dances. I quickly look around for dry twigs, small ones and large.

Soon, there is a fire. The wolves are frightened, but I calm them. I dip my finger in the small pond and let a single drop of water fall on the thin topstone. It sizzles. I pick up two eggs and crack them on top. Some of it drips over the side, but most of it stays there. It is quickly cooked and I use some small stones to toss it onto a broad leaf. I quickly crack another two eggs. When the first two are cool, I call forth two of the pack. They eat greedily, but gratefully. The second two eggs goes to the next two wolves. The other two wolves are the smallest and so the last to come forward. They share one and wolf and I share the last one. It is not a lot, but they are all grateful. It feels like we are kin.

We lie on the grass. My thoughts turn to what I am doing. Where am I going? I have worked hard with Mother. But am I arriving anywhere? What am I to do? What am I to become?

I cannot be a miller. That is certain. I am not strong in that way and I would not like to do the same thing every day. And I could not farm animals. I eat flesh sometimes, but I am happier with vegetables and fruit. I could not farm crops. I would get tired of taking care of them. I can make things. I made the wolf's head. Perhaps I could make other things and sell them at Dol market. But would people give me anything for them? And if they did, what of it? I do not want coin. Anything else they give me, I can get myself. And what do I want anyway? My tunic is getting small, but I can get another one from the village. One day soon I will need a man's clothes. But there are men there who have clothes they do not need. Perhaps women whose husbands have died in senseless battle against the brothers they did not know their enemies were.

No, I am to be none of these things. What can I do? I can bless the bone fire. Perhaps I can do other things for the village, too. Mother has taught me a little about the healing plants and she says she will teach me more. But she says I can find out for myself if I want, by turning on my sight and talking to the forest. I can ask what is good for healing a problem and the plants will tell me.

Healing and helping. They are good things. I want to lead a good life, like John the miller, but not by being a miller. That is it! A good life is one that you were born to live. Whatever I do, if I do it well and help other people, it is a good life. Then I will rest easy with our Lord. At least for a time. Or perhaps not. If we rest with our Lord, what happens to those poor souls who have not heard of our Lord? No, going to our Lord cannot be right, in spite of what the Father always says in church. I know that there is something else after the death of the body. I am certain that one thing that will happen is that I will look at how I lived my life. After that, I do not know. Perhaps people work in the land of mist. But it cannot be hard work, because they have no body. It is only because we have bodies that we have difficulties. Perhaps people plan where they are going to be born next when they come back here.

These are mysteries, and probably not ones I need to worry about while I am alive. I am just happy to be here at the moment. And, when I help others, it is like I am helping myself. After the blessing of the bone fire with Ulph, I was tired for a time, but afterwards, I felt wonderful. It is as if, in blessing, I was blessed. Here is wisdom, lad, I imagine Mother saying: What you give is what you get. So give love. I want to give love more than anything. Perhaps, in return, I will receive the love of the villagers. This makes me wonder if I will ever marry. I would like to give love and get love. But I do not think I will. I think my love has to go to more than one person.

Without warning, I am frightened! Something might happen to Mother. When Mother dies, I will have to take over. That means I will have to teach someone else. If I do not, when times are bad in the far future, when I am the sweating man with the big hands, people will not know what to do to make things better, so that I can become the girl, talking to the machine which gives her water. How are things continued if there is death too soon?

I must discuss this with Mother. It is a very important thing. She must have thought of this. She must know the answer.

Wolf's ears prick up. He stands in front of me. His deep, dark eyes gaze into mine. Then he is gone. The pack go with him. I think they have heard a large creature moving through the forest. A bit of egg is not enough for a wolf.

I lie down. I have to decide if I am going to stay here tonight. I will. I have a lot to think about.

The Father in the church once said that when he talks to us, he reads. One Sun day, when I was leaving the church, he spoke to me. To me! He had never done that before. He blessed me and my work. I thanked him. Then I was brave. I said, 'Please, Father. What is "read"?' He told me to come back the next day after the mill. I did and he explained it to me. He even showed me the book. I saw strange little drawings. He said that each drawing meant a sound. So if I said something, he could write it. Then, he did a wonderful thing. He took a small piece of paper and a pen. He wrote my name. He explained each sound to me. Then, even more wonderful, he gave me the piece of paper! I ran, ran home and showed my mother. She did not understand why I was excited. A miller does not need to read.

I think it would be wonderful to write and read. If I could do that, I could learn so much. And I could write down everything Mother has told me. That way, it would not be forgotten if I went back to the mist before I could tell anyone else.

That is what I want to do next. Perhaps Mother can read. Perhaps she will teach me.

I climb on the branch I found last time. I turn on my sight and look at the stars for a little while. Then I turn it off and sleep.

Chapter 7

The next morning, I wake in fear. I do not know why. I have no reason to be afraid. I am also very sad.

Where did this fear come from? Did I hear a forest beast in my sleep? Perhaps wolf is back, but I am not afraid of wolf.

I can feel it in my middle. It is strong.

I stop and breathe. I turn on my mist sight. Perhaps there is something in the mist. I look round. The sun is coming up. There is the light of the forest. Tiny water creatures swim quickly in the water that they are.

I try something. In my thoughts and feels, I call the man who was here before. He drifts in from the mist on my right. I greet him. He greets me.

'I am frightened and sad. Do you know why?'

'Yes,' he says.

'Please tell me.'

He has a slight smile. It is always there. I like it, but if it was in a living person, I would not trust him. But this one I do trust. He is part of me.

'All people have a time that they are frightened. It is when everything seems without hope. It is when the whole of life seems without hope. This is natural. You need to make a decision. The best decision is the one that takes you on your own, special way. Your way through the forest of life is not anybody else's way. People become sad because they do not know how to be like other people. You must decide how to be more like yourself.'

'How do I do that?'

'I cannot help you. That is your decision. Just know that there is no wrong decision. If it turns out you think it is wrong, that means you are a step closer to being right. People have to make mistakes to grow.'

I think about these things. Then I have a question.

'What is fear? Why do we have it?'

He has that smile still.

'Fear is useful. Fear makes us stop.'

'What do you mean?'

'If you are carrying in the mill, but you are not looking where you are going, you might suddenly turn round and find yourself in front of the moving topstone. It is dangerous. There is fear, so you stop. That is quick and natural. You do not decide. It simply happens. But sometimes, fear makes people stop in life. They see life as frightening, so they stop experiencing it. They stop growing. They do not know what they are frightened of, but they stop anyway.'

'Is that what is happening to me?'

'No. There is another kind of stopping, another root of fear. It is fear that you cannot be yourself and cannot make a difference. You see the sadness of the world and feel powerless to change it. What you do not see is that you are not powerless to change it. You think that you can only change your own experience of the world. But if you change yourself, the world around you will change. Then, the world around those people in your world will slowly start to change. This way, change starts to go across the land. And you are not the only person like you. There are others who see, others who have people like Mother. They are everywhere. As your sight develops, you will be able to link with them.'

'So what do I do?'

'Believe.'

He disappears into the mist.

Believe? What does that mean? Believe what? In what?

The sun is full up, so I set off back. I must discuss some things with Mother.

She is picking healing plants when I arrive. She sees me and smiles, but continues picking. I offer to help, but she says I will get in the way. So I sit by the pool.

Then, I see the stone. Last time, Mother gave me a drink before I sat. I want to know what will happen if I just sit. So I move over to the stone. I step on and sit.

There is a hum, like miller John near the end of a spring day. I turn on my sight. There is light everywhere. I sit in a shaft of light. The light has a quality like mist, but it is bright. Like real mist when the sun reflects off the millpond. I relax. I feel my back easing. It is better now than before, but the light helps a lot. After a short time, the pain is all but gone.

I step off and go to lie next to the pond. I feel light, like a cat.

When Mother is done, she carries her basket into the house. After a short time, I follow. I watch her put the plants in their places. She seems slower than before. Just as I have a lightness, she seems to have a heaviness.

'Are you well, Mother?'

'Aye, lad. Well enough. Just old.'

I feel sad for a moment. It would be so hard without her.

'Mother, I need to ask you something.'

'Wait, then.' She is making plant water and does not like anything to stop that. She brings two mugs over. I realise I am thirsty. And hungry.

I sip my drink. It is good, as always.

'Mother. Just as you have taught me these mysteries, I feel I must tell them to another.'

'That's good. I knew you would get there in the end.'

'But Mother, we are not here forever. Soon it will be your time to go into the mist. I am frightened. Not because of that. I know I will be fine. And you. But, oh, Mother, what would happen if I went into the mist before I told another the things you have told me? How would things go on? What would happen to the village?'

She sips her drink, looking at me over the cup's top.

'That is good. And that is what I must teach you. The men are coming from across the sea soon. Mayhap everyone will pass into the mist. The men will take everything. You remember. They will keep our land for over a thousand years, but we will get it back. But, aye, what if they kill those who keep the ancient knowledge? That is what we must talk about next.'

I look at her. I know better than to speak. The light of the mist is talking through her.

She hands me her cup and I go to wash them. It is autumn, but not cold in the sun. I decide to bathe. The water is so cold, but good. I wash my feet and face and hair. It is getting long. I must take a knife to it later. As I wash my face, I feel tiny hairs. I have not noticed them before.

I stand and dry in the sun, rubbing my body. I slip my tunic on. It is small now.

I go inside.

'Sit you down, lad.'

I sit. Mother has a box next to her on the floor. I have seen it before, but I have not asked her about it. She opens it. She takes out a piece of paper and a piece of charcoal with a point.

'You can learn to read if you like, but there is no need. What you know is not in books. And you can learn to write. But people have different tongues in this land. To the south and west, there is a land where they speak differently. You must go there one day. Wise people are there. Aye, wiser than me. You might have to learn their tongue. But think, lad. Tongues change. If you write down the ancient knowledge, future folk might not be able to read it. There is a better tongue.'

She takes the charcoal and makes a sign on the paper. It is the sign of the cross. I cross myself when I see it.

'Signs, lad. If you can learn signs, you can make signs. Signs have meaning, aye, and power. You can put all the wisdom into signs. If future folk see it, they might not be able to read the signs, but the signs have wisdom in them and folk like you and me can pull it out. See this sign?'

'Yes,' I say. 'It is the cross of Jesus.'

'Oh, yes, they stole it alright. Because it is a powerful sign. But it is much older than Jesus. Look.'

She points to the top of the cross.

'This is the light, high up, above the mist. It comes down to this world.' She draws her finger down to the bottom. 'Then the light spreads out into the world. Left and right.' She draws the crosspiece.

'Now, this is you, lad. You can draw down the light and spread it out. But what if we do this?'

She draws a circle around the sign and makes the old cross.

'You get the old cross,' I say.

'Aye, but what is this ring? A ring has no beginning and no end. It is everything, every possibility. This is you again. You can draw down the light and spread it around in an endless number of ways. The ring also contains you. The light of the spirit world wants to experience everything, so it must become everything and do everything. This ring shows the endless ways in which love can be.'

I consider this. It is a wonder.

Over the day, Mother shows me so many signs. She tells me what they mean. She tells me how they can be used. How they can be used to show things, and how they can be used to create things. Some are simple, like the three-lined box. Some take a lot of simple signs and make complicated ones. It is simple. It is complicated. It is wonderful. An equal-armed cross means the things we can touch. A ring means spirit. If you make a ring and put a cross underneath it, it means spirit is more important than the things of the world. I like that. Mother says that it is also the sign for a woman. If you put the cross above the ring, it is the sign for a man. They usually think the world is more important than spirit. She cackles when she says this. But, says Mother, we all need both.

The most wondrous sign she shows me is the last one. It is very complicated, but she takes me through it patiently. One part shows this world. Another part shows thoughts, another feels. One part shows the mist world. And there are other parts to it too. She shows me how all the parts are connected. Then she points at things and tells me the mistakes people make in this world and why they make them. It is a wonder. I will keep it in my thoughts always. When I speak to people, I will be able to use this wisdom to help them.

She spends the whole day talking. I am not tired. I am excited.

At night, when I can finally sleep, I see the signs in my dreams.

Chapter 8

The next morning, I wake with the sun. It is still not cold, even though it has been some time since Samhain. As I wake fully, I am aware of being watched. I look over at the table. Mother is sitting there, staring down at me.

'What do you know of your father?' she asks.

That makes me sit upright. I am about to answer, but she continues.

'Go. Wash. When you come back, tell me everything.'

I do so at once. The forest animals are quieter. The rain has stopped, but the trees are still dripping. I pull off my tunic. The water is colder now. Mist hangs low over the pond. As I float, I look to the left and right. Through the mist, I can see the forest way. I drift around and see the house. Mother has lit a fire. It will burn through until Beltane.

The thought of fire and food makes me move. I wash my face. It feels good. Mother has told me that it is important to keep the body clean. But it is also important to keep the mist body clean. The body can be washed with water. The mist body has to be washed with mist water. That is made with our thought pictures. Each day, when I bathe, I imagine my mist body lying in a pool and the pool is taking away the dirt in the mist around me.

I get out. The mist is cold. I rub my body, then slip on my tunic.

Inside, it is warm. There is a covered part at the back of the house, full of logs. Each log is too big for Mother's hearth, so I cut them, a few each day.

I smell mushrooms. And hot drink.

We sit and take our fill. The forest mushrooms are so good. Mother has shown me which ones are good and which are bad. The bad ones can kill, she says. Sometimes, bad people take the bad ones and feed them to people they do not like. I think that is terrible. If people knew that they come back and everything that they do to people is done to them, the world would be better.

When I have washed the bowls, I sit with Mother.

'Now, lad. Tell me all you know.'

I pause. I am not sure what to say, I know so little.

'I do not remember him well. When I was not much more than a babe, he left to fight a war. He did not come back, so I think he died.'

Mother's eyes narrow.

'No, lad. That is not what happened. Settle back. This is a long tale.'

'About a year before you were born, at Beltane, there was a meeting of the villages from around the forest. This place where we live is on a strip of land jutting out into the sea. It is only a day's walk across. There are ten villages hereabouts. You know yours and Dol. The others are beyond Dol. So that day, the heads of the villages, including Thomas, met in Dol, because it is the easiest one for everyone to reach. They talked about strange things that had been happening. The weather was strange. Snow in May and such. Crows were everywhere. Thunder rumbled at Yule tide, but there was no rain. And other things. You don't have to be me to know that signs like these are not good. But nobody knew what it meant.

'Some thought it just bad luck. The folk at the churches said we should pray harder. Others came up with similar nonsense. I knew what was happening alright, but nobody asked me. Trouble was, I don't have the power to work against something like that. I had to get word to Hywel. And the trouble with that was he lived in that land I told you of, to the south and west. There was only one way I knew to get word to him.

'I walked to Dol and asked when Kevin would be coming next. Kevin the traveller. Kevin the storyteller. He brings news of the world outside, together with some of his own nonsense. If I could get hold of him, I could get him to take a message to

Hywel. He goes to Hywel's home about once a year. So, in Dol, they said that Kevin had last been there at Imbolc and said he would return a moon after Beltane. I was in luck. I returned to Dol just before the moon after Beltane and back again every day until I found him. We've spoken before. I know his nonsense, and he knows I know, and he tells me I'm a wicked woman, but we tolerate each other. Bit of playfulness, if you want to know. So I tell him he has to get to Hywel. He's a bit corn dolly at first, stiff and dumb and unsmiling. But I press on him how important it is. So, eventually, he agrees and asks for the message. I say, "Tell Hywel: 'Mother needs you.' That's all." I thought even a simpleton like Kevin could remember such a short message.

'You see, Hywel and me, we know each other well. He knew I would never call him to come all that way, maybe a moon's travel, unless it was important. Now, I was somewhat surprised, knowing Kevin as I did, when Hywel turned up on my doorstep about two moons later.

'I welcomed my old friend and sat him down. He told me what was happening in his land, and farther afield. Then he asks what's happening here. So I say, "Strange weather, strange behaviour. Until just before Yule, things were as they had been forever. Now, things are not right. Folk getting angry. Folk getting sad. And most folk just talk about coin. As if that's all that matters. I ask them what they'll do with the coin when they get it and they look at me queer, as if I've asked them why they breathe."

'Hywel looks at me. Then he says, "You think it's a glamour." I nod at him. "A powerful one," I say. He goes off into one of his journeys inside. It's always best to leave him to it. So while he's travelling, I make him more plant water. When he's back, his eyes are all dark. He nods. He drinks his water. He stands. "Right then," he says. "I'd best get to it."

'So he did what he does and the glamour lifted. His magic is very powerful. He can do things I have never even thought of.

The ten village folk were like they were waking from a dream. He called a meeting and told them what had happened. They were delighted and arranged a feast for him. Now, lad, it gets interesting for you.

'At the feast, with meat stew for all and drink flowing like water, Hywel spotted this woman across the room. And she spotted him. And I spotted them spotting each other. I think, "It must be spring". Hehe! So they got together and, after a few days, they fell in love. Hywel decided to stay in the village and, after a time, they got married. First in the church, then with one of Hywel's own ceremonies. She was living with her sister at the time—she's long dead now—so they couldn't live there. So Hywel built them a small house on the edge of the village. The villagers were more than happy to have him here and everyone helped them build the house. And all was well.

'After a year, they had a baby. When the babe is a few years old, Hywel gets word of trouble of some sort back in his home. His villagers needed his skills. He struggled to decide, but his wife was a good woman and told him that, if people needed help, he should go. So he did.'

I listen in silence. My plant water is not touched. I have a question, although I think I know the answer.

'And the girl and the babe?'

'You know. The girl sadly passed back into the mist. The babe sits before me.'

I have another question. It is more important. I do not know the answer to this one.

'Mother, what became of Hywel?'

She smiles. 'As far as I know, he's still alive. Still living in his village. Still the greatest power for good in this land.'

She gets up and goes outside. She has left me to think. My father. Alive? A boy needs a mother, but a growing boy needs a father. Mothers teach us how to be, and fathers teach us how to do. Will he come here again? There is no reason why he should.

I know what I must do.

When Mother returns, she has a happy-sad face.

'I have been to see Master Thomas. He knows you'll be leaving us for a while. The full moon is next Sun day. A good time to leave.'

I want to laugh. I want to cry. I understand Mother's face.

Then I am frightened. I have never left the village, except to come here. And such a long way. Where will I sleep? How will I find food? And how will I know the way. Mother sees these thoughts in my mist.

'Fear not, lad. The mist light will keep you safe. I saw this day coming and I made Kevin give me this.'

She goes in her box and takes out a roll of paper. She unrolls it on the table. She tells me that it is a map. She points at our village and the forest. There is a way leading south. I see signs by the side of the ways. She says they are numbers. Quickly she shows me the signs for the numbers. She says the numbers on the map are days. Two days on this way. Take the right path. Three days on that way. Take the right path. She shows me signs for inns and the homes of good people. And she shows me the home of Hywel.

'Let me show you something.' She pulls over her box once again and opens it.

She takes out a piece of metal. It is polished well and is very shiny.

'Have you ever seen yourself?'

'No, Mother.'

'Then look.'

She holds up the metal in front of me. I see myself for the first time. I have seen my face in water, but this is different. It is so clear. I have hair sticking out everywhere. I have all my teeth and they are almost straight. I thought I had beard hair, but I see none. A small nose. Big ears. But mostly, I see the eyes. My eyes are big. Really big. And they are a strong blue. I smile and the face in the plate smiles. I think it is quite a good face.

But it is still the face of a small boy. And I have a huge journey ahead.

'That, lad, is the face of a good person. Aye, and a strong one. You might not think so sometimes, but you are strong. Not in the way of John the miller, maybe, but strong where it's important. You can do anything. This journey will show you that.'

A week later, we go to the village. I am wearing the Ulph figure. Mother and I took it to the stones and put some of Ulph's mist into it. I put it onto a leather strip and hung it around my neck. I feel him like a warm glow in my heart.

Mother carries a cloth full of things. When we arrive in the centre of the village, by the well, everyone is gathered there. Master Thomas steps forward.

'Young Master, we are sad you are leaving, but we know it is best for you and best for the village. We know you will return. So we wanted to give you some things to help you on your long journey.'

He hands me a tunic. It is bigger and made of good cloth. It is a boy's tunic, but I am happy. It will reach near to my knees. There are no leggings or shoes, but I can manage as I am for some time. As if reading my thoughts, Master Thomas says, 'We wanted to get you shoes and leggings. It'll be cold soon. But we could not afford the cloth or leather.' I smile at him. 'But we did make you this. Well, Mary made it.'

He hands me a bag. It, too, is fine cloth. I put it over my head with the strap on my left shoulder. The bag hangs down to the right. I am overjoyed. I have never owned a bag before. I have never owned anything before. I see Mary. I smile at her and nod. Then I look away. I am still shy after all. My shyness seems to make her very happy. Girls are strange sometimes.

Mother takes me to one side and opens her bundle cloth. There is the map, a few days' food, a skin of water, some healing plants, some smoke dust with the good smell and some candles.

It is a good bundle. Then she tells me she has one more thing for me. She turns to Master Thomas and nods. He goes round the back of the well and I see him bend to pick something up.

It is a staff! As tall as me. He hands it to Mother.

'This is your staff, lad,' she says. I look at it. There are signs carved all along its length. The top is wider and in the shape of a flame. 'I have put into it the most powerful magic I know. It will protect you. Do not let anyone else touch it. Up to now, it is mine, so I must give it to you proper.'

She holds it up in the air and mutters something. Clouds roll across the sky. A rumble of thunder. A brief shower. A wind picks up and dies. Then the sun comes out and all is silent.

Mother mutters a few more words. Then, louder, she says, 'And so I give unto you this staff. May it protect and guide you and work for you as you need it.'

She hands me the staff. I feel a tingle everywhere. I shudder. Then I breathe and all is calm.

I take a breath. I look at Mother. I look at the villagers. I am still a little frightened, but I am happy.

I turn around. I look at the way ahead, the way I have never travelled. One step. Then I turn. I raise my arms, the staff in my right hand, and bless the villagers and the village. Then I turn and take ten more steps. I turn. They are still watching me. I nod, turn, and start my journey.

As I walk, I keep turning. They are still watching. I wave. They all wave back. I keep walking. I keep turning. When the village is almost out of sight, I stop. This is it. I am leaving home. A few more steps and there is no more village. There is only forward. I take those few steps. I turn. The village is gone.

I am alone.

The way is easy at first. Through the edge of the forest and out into green land. The land is beautiful. This place is so green. When a shower starts, I do not mind. It is soon gone and the sun comes out again. The way is flat and I am enjoying the day.

After half a day, I see a hill up ahead. The way climbs up and over. At the top, I look back. I cannot see the village, but I think I see the forest. Turning forward, I reach the top of the hill. The land sweeps down ahead of me. There is green everywhere. And brown forests where the trees have lost their leaves. And darker green ones with those trees which keep theirs. I see the way winding ahead.

As the sun lowers, I start to wonder where I will sleep. The map says there is no inn on the first day, so I look for a likely spot outside.

I decide to use the sight. I turn it on. When I look at my staff, I almost drop it! It is on fire! There is red mist around the tip. Lower down, it is strong blue. When I calm myself, I look around. I ask the question. Where can I sleep? I look around again. Off to the right, there is a flash in the mist. I turn off the sight, step off the path and walk in that direction. It is a small wood. When I get there, I look around. Trees. Wet, rotting leaves on the ground. But one patch looks different. I scrape at the leaves. There is a framework of thin branches underneath. I lift one branch and the whole framework comes up. Underneath, there is a hole! It is a lupus hole; wolf hole. It is for travellers who are seen by a pack. They can hide here. I jump in. I pull the framework down. There is a leather strip with a peg on the end. I push the peg into the ground.

I am tired. There is just enough room for me to stretch out. A man would have to curl up. At first, it is chill but, after a time, it is warmer. I go in my bag and find a little bread and cheese. I take a little water from the skin. Within a short time, I am sleepy. Although I am short enough to stretch out, I curl up and put an arm round my knees.

Next morning, at first, I am confused, because it is still dark. Then I remember where I am. I take out the peg and push up the framework. It is dawn. And it is raining. Not hard, but I will be wet quickly. Still, I have a journey to make.

The rain soon clears and I am back on the way heading south. I am very hungry. I pass through a farm. A dog comes out and barks at me. I talk to him, using a little mist magic, and he calms. The farmer appears and greets me.

'Good day, lad. Heading south?'

'Good day, Master. I am. I have a long journey.'

'Is that right? Have you broken your fast?'

'No, sir. I have little food.'

'Then come. We are eating.'

'God bless you, Master. I do not deserve such kindness.'

'Nonsense, lad. We must all help a traveller in this world.'

In the small farmhouse, I meet the farmer's wife. There are four children. Two girls, two boys. One girl and one boy are small, about eight summers. The other girl is older, but has not grown big in front yet. The other boy is about my age. They look friendly.

The food is wonderful and most well come. They give me two eggs, bread and cheese. I have a new feeling. I am full. I cannot eat any more. I give the biggest thanks I can and God bless them all for their kindness. I ask if there is anything I can do in return. The farmer says I can clean out the chickens.

The older children go off in different directions, to their own tasks. I cut across the mud ground to a chicken box. It is well built. I greet the chickens and they let me clean up. The farmer looks when I have finished and he is pleased.

He gives me a little bread and cheese for my journey. It is far more than I need or deserve. There are good people in this world. I smile, thank him again, and head back to the path. When I am half the distance to the way, I turn and bless the farm, the farmer and his family. May they have some good luck, I ask the mist light.

Back on the way, I am happy. It is still flat and an easy journey. The rain has stopped, but it is still cloudy. Smells are on the air. The smell of decaying leaves. I like it. And smoke from some unseen fire. It is a good journey so far.

Before the sun is at its highest, I see something. At the side of the way. There is a huge beast standing there. It has four legs. It is a little like a cow, but thinner, with a long nose and much taller. It has a wide back, with something made of leather on it. The beast looks fierce. I do not want to go near it, but it is next to the way and I must pass it. Then I see something else.

Leaning against a tree, there is a man. He looks hurt. I find courage and go to him. There is a cut on his head. I touch him. He groans. I take out my skin which the farmer filled. I hold it up to the man's mouth. He drinks a little. There is blood in his eyes, and he is too weak to open them. I go in the bag and take out some plants which are good for cuts. Mother has put in some strips of cloth and some wider squares. I put water on one of them and clean the cut and his eyes. The man moans again. I mash up a plant and put it on the cut. Then I tie one of the strips around his head.

I sit back and turn on my sight. His mist is thin. He is weak. I take my staff and hold it. I call down light mist and place my hand on his middle. Light mist pours through the staff, through me and into the man. I see his mist getting stronger and lighter. I clear away the red mist around his cut and pour a little white mist into it. He makes a sound. It is still a groan, but stronger.

I turn off the sight and look at the man properly. He is dressed in a fine tunic and warm leggings. I look down at my bare, dirty legs and feet. His shoes are leather and well cut. I see he has a knife. He is wealthy, possibly a lord. That makes me frightened for a moment.

I hold his hand and wish him well. After a time, he wakes and blinks. Then he sees me. He snatches back his hand and puts it to his head. He feels the cloth strip. I see him think for a moment.

'Did you do this?'

'If it please you, Master, I did. You were asleep. The cut is deep.'

He pats his hand on my shoulder. 'Thank you. You did well, lad. You have some healing?'

'A little, Master.'

'Where did you learn?'

'From the wise woman in the village, Master.'

'She taught you well. I feel strong.'

I risk a smile. He smiles back. He tries to rise, but is a little dizzy. I try to catch him, but he sits. Then he tries again. With a little help, he makes it up. He leans against the tree for a moment. Then he nods at me and walks towards the beast.

I dare say, 'If it please you, Master. What is that great beast?'

He stops and turns. He sees where I am looking.

'That is my horse, lad.' I continue to look at the beast.

'Master, is it fierce?'

He gives out a great laugh.

'Have you never seen a horse, lad?'

'No, Master. Is it for milk?'

He laughs again, even louder.

'No, lad. For riding.'

I cannot think what he means. You could not ride on such a beast. It is too big.

He asks, 'Where are you heading, lad?'

'South, Master. I go to the sign of the sheep, then turn right.'

'Ah. Off to the land in the west.'

'Yes, Master.'

'Well, you deserve something for helping me. I can take you to the sign of the sheep.'

I do not know what he means, so I just say, 'Thank you, Master.'

He moves to the horse. He takes a strip of leather connected to its head. He holds this and walks towards me. The horse follows. It is so big!

He puts his foot in something and, in a moment, he is on the horse. I look up at him. He looks a long way away. He leans down towards me and holds out his hands.

'Give me your hand, lad.'

I do as he bids. He pulls. He is very strong. In a moment, I am behind him. I am terrified. It is so high. He sees my eyes. I think he understands.

'Fear not, lad. The horse does as I bid him. Hold tight to me.'

I lay my staff on my lap and hold onto his jerkin. He makes a click with his mouth and the beast moves. I feel very unsafe and throw my arms round him. After a time, I feel safer. It is wondrous up here.

'A little faster, I think. Hold on!'

I hold him and the horse moves faster. I am terrified again. I hold him tight. I close my eyes. After some time, and when I see that I have not fallen off, I open them again.

'All well, lad?'

I struggle to speak. 'Quite well, Master.'

He laughs.

'Well, hold on again.'

He kicks the horse and it goes even faster. I do not like this.

We travel like this for half the morning. Then we reach a village. He slows and takes the horse to a long bucket filled with water. The horse drinks deep. When it stops, he takes us slowly to a place on the other side of the village. A muscled man comes out.

'Good day, Master. Check the shoes?'

'If you would.'

I almost laugh at the idea of a horse wearing shoes. The man lifts each leg in turn.

'All well, Master.'

He nods and tosses the man a coin.

'Thank you, Master.'

And we are travelling again.

We stay at inns for two nights. The Master pays for food and a bed.

At the end of the third day, we arrive at the sign of the sheep. We stay there another night.

In the morning, Master bids me good journey. I thank him and bid him the same. He says he is going to the capital. I do not know what that means, what that is, or where. This land is so big.

I look at the map. In three days, I have covered a distance which would take me most of half a moon to walk.

I look back up the way, thinking how far from my home I am. I look the other ways and try to imagine what wonders there are in the capital. Then I take the way west. Another few days and I will be there. I think of my father and that gives me strength.

Towards the end of the day, the way gets hilly. Up and down. It is tiring. I do not meet many people. No men with horses. I am short of food and water, but I am sure I will find something soon.

After noon, I see some men walking towards me. As we pass, I smile a little, but they do not speak. They stop.

'Travelling far, boy?'

'Yes, Master.'

He turns to his two friends and mutters something. One of the others nods.

'I like your staff.'

'Thank you, Master.'

'I would like to have it.'

I do not know what to say. I want to be kind, but it is my staff. Unless I can...

'Give it to me.'

I hold the staff and whisper to it. I ask the fire to come down and be felt by anyone but me. I hand it to the man.

He screams and drops it. 'What is that?'

They look at the staff. They look at each other. They look at me. I make myself big with mist. I am not big, but they will think I am. They look, but they cannot see. But they feel.

The one who took the staff says, 'Pardon, young Master. I meant nothing. C'mon lads. C'mon.'

They turn and walk. Quickly.

I collect my staff. Not everybody in the world is good.

Later, as the sun is going down and I have just gone over a hill, I hear a noise behind me. It reminds me of the topstone moving in John's mill. I turn. Coming over the hill is a cart. It is like the cart I had to pull to take bags of flour to the village. But this one is much bigger. And it is being pulled by a horse! I am not as frightened as I was with the other horse. This one is slower and has more hair around its eyes and neck and feet. An old man sits on the cart. It is piled with things. I cannot see clearly what they are.

He stops the horse. He smiles and nods. I smile and nod in return. I wait until he speaks to me before I speak.

'Good day, young lad.'

'Good day, Master.'

'Where you headin'?' He has a strange way of saying words.

I tell him the name of the place where Hywel lives.

'Don't know that one. But hop up and I'll take you as far as I can.'

'God bless you, Master.'

I take out the map. There are inns marked. As we move, I show him. There is an inn with a sign of a wheat sheaf. I tell him.

'I know that one. Be stayin' there tonight.'

I tell him of the three inns between the sign of the wheat sheaf and the village I am heading for. He knows them all, but is only going as far as the second one, the sign of the straw man. It would be wonderful if I could get there. The cart is only a little faster than walking, but so much easier.

He seems a friendly man, so I have courage.

'May it please you, Master. You have shown me enough kindness. Could I beg for more and ask you to take me there.'

He smiles. 'Of course, lad. Be company for an old man.'

'And, Master, what may I do for you in return?'

I know that things must be in balance.

'Nothing I need doin'. Unless,' he chuckles, 'you can do anythin' for an achin' back.'

I wonder. Will he be open to things?

'Begging your pardon, Master, but do you believe in the old ways?'

He looks at me sharp. 'That I do, boy. You're in the land of the old ways. Them Christians tried their thing here, but it didn't hold. Course, there are churches and that, but the old ways hold sway.'

'Then you know that the forest folk have healing skills?'

'That I do. What of it?'

I take a breath. 'I was taught in a forest dell.'

He gives me that look again. Then a slight smile. When he speaks, it is slow with something. Interest? Wonder?

'Were you now?' he mutters.

I give a small smile and a nod. I ask him to stop for a moment. All is silent. There was a slight breeze, but it has dropped.

I turn on my sight and look at his back. Low down, near the bottom, there is red mist. I pull it out with my hands, feeling the hot mist. I cast it into the earth. The earth can take it and clean it and return it to the land to become trees and plants. Then, one hand holds the staff and the other is on his back. Cooling blue-green mist comes down like soft dust, through my staff, through me and into his back. He gasps. I let it go on for a while, making sure the red is made calm and the hole is filled. I come back to myself and remove my hand.

He looks ahead. He feels his back with both hands. He looks at me sharp again. Then he give a huge grin. Then he starts laughing.

'You did it, lad! The first time for many moons with no pain.' He slaps me on the back. He is none too gentle.

'Hahaha! Do I believe in the old ways? Hahaha!'

I smile. I have done some good.

His spirits are uplifted as we continue and he chats away. He tells me of his family and his farm. He has fruit and vegetables in the back. A good harvest. He is on his way to the village markets to sell them. He asks me to reach back into the nearest bag and get him an apple. Then he says I can have one too. He is kindly, and the apple is sweet and delicious. Even better than the ones Mother found, I think.

The day passes quickly and we reach the sign of the wheat sheaf. I tell him I have no coin, so I will sleep with the horses. He says nonsense and I am to stay with him. We have food and drink. And then we go to our room, exhausted. There is a straw mattress on the floor. We are asleep straight away.

In the morning, I wake with the sun.

After two days, we reach the sign of the straw man. It is wonderful how far I have come and how quickly. I have met so many helpful people. There is always good in the world.

In the morning, I say fare well and God bless you to the kindly man. He goes the other way and I head west. Only a few more days. If I do not meet another traveller with a cart, I know I will not get to the final inn in one day, so I will have to sleep under the stars. I like that, but it is growing colder.

I walk at a good pace. It is hard to believe I will be with my father the day after tomorrow. When the sun is high, I stop and have one of the apples the old man gave me. I have some water left, but it is nearly gone. Farther down the road, passing through a farm, I meet a young maid with milk pails. I nod to her. She nods, but does not speak. It would not be right to speak to her, so I just smile.

The land is green. Somehow, it is greener here than it was before. Perhaps because I am facing the sun.

I meet no other people that day. As the sun gets low, I look around for somewhere to sleep. I think I will need shelter. The clouds are dark and rain comes with dark clouds. I decide to ask the light mist again and turn on my sight. Everything is sparking like stars, but I see no big light to show me the way. Sometimes, the mist does not help us because we have to help ourselves.

Eventually, when it is near dark, I sit by the way side and lean against the bank. It is cold now. I am shivering. It is so cold I cannot sleep. I rub myself. I cannot get warm. The wind is stronger. There is nothing I can do but keep walking. I am near the top of a hill. Perhaps if I can get lower down, it will not be as cold.

I walk, but it is dark. The waning gibbous is hidden by cloud. I can just see the way ahead and keep going. After a time, I feel I am going downhill. It is not as windy. I look around, but it is full dark now. Off the way, I think I see a tree. I head towards it. I am right. There is just a breeze now, but I sit on the side away from the wind. The walk has made me a little warmer. I lean against the bark and sleep, wake, sleep, wake until dawn.

As I set off, I feel tired. But I sit and eat the last apple given to me by the cart man. It is sweet and my spirits rise a little. I set off again. Tomorrow should see me with my father.

I am not sure why I want to see him. I do not really remember him. There is nothing I can think of that he can do for me, or I for him. But I think we want to know where we come from. That way, we have a clearer idea of how to live. And it helps us know where we are going.

I look at the map. The final inn before my father's village is over a half day away. All being well, I will be inside before night. This time, I will have to sleep with the horses.

The day passes well. I meet a few folk on the road. Most are heading towards the wheat sheaf, but I share the way with a farmer for a time. As he heads off up into the hills to care for his sheep, he offers me a little of his bread. I bless and thank him.

I am on my own again. Midday comes and goes. I know I am on the right way, but it is hilly and I cannot see very far ahead. Eventually, I crest a hill and see the inn. It is to the side of the way, next to a small wood. The trees have lost most of their leaves.

I find the stable and look for the stable man. He is not there. I look around the back of the stable. Not there either. I dare not go inside the inn. They would not be happy if a boy entered, and one without coin at that. They would chase me out. I decide to wait for the stable man and sit near the door. I take off my bag. My shoulder is a little sore. I lay it down next to my staff.

I doze. I do not mean to, but it is a little warmer now and I did not sleep much last night. I am woken by a noise. It is a horse approaching. It clops in. Another big beast. I stand to be respectful to the man riding it. His boots are long and made of good leather. He wears fine clothes and a cloak. I know he is a gentleman, even a lord. That means he is a man of power and control. As I notice this, I go into a daydream, remembering Mother. Each time we come back to this world, we learn and, hopefully, get better. And we have to learn different things as we go. Worldly power and money are things for people to learn when they are not very familiar with the world and how it works. Mother says I should try to treat them kindly, because they are children, in a way. He shouts at me and I am startled, by him and by the horse.

'Take the rein, lad, and put her inside.'

I do not know what to do. I have never guided a horse. I do not know what a 'rein' is. I am frightened, so I stop.

'Are you simple, boy? I said take her!' he shouts.

I take hold of the strip of leather which goes to the thing in its mouth, just as I had seen the other rider do. The man jumps off. He tosses me a coin. I thank him and he walks inside. I pull the leather strip, gently. The beast takes a step. I send a kind thought to the beast and a picture of a warm stable. She makes a strange noise, but starts walking. I hold the leather still while I open the stable door. Then I walk her inside. I see two other horses there and guide the horse so she is in the next section. I wrap the leather around a piece of wood, in the same manner as the other horses.

I go outside, quite pleased that I have handled a horse. I look at the coin he gave me. It is enough for food and a bed! I quickly collect my bag and staff.

Before I go inside, I take a breath, and draw down light and breathe out to make my mist body larger. I hope they will notice me and not a young boy. I open the door. It is heavy and I have to push hard. It is warm inside. A wood fire is burning. An old man sits near it, warming his hands. Beyond the fire, two men sit at a table drinking. The landlord sees me.

He comes forward. He has on a dirty apron. He is a big man with a beard. I smile a little. It is difficult, because he is very tall and looks stern.

'Now then, boy. What is it?'

He has a loud voice. I tremble a little.

'Please you, Master. I would like food and a bed.'

He holds out his hand. I place the coin in it. He nods.

'Sit you down, lad.'

There is a small table with a stool between the door and the fire. I place my bag underneath and lay my staff on the floor. I am soon warm. The landlord brings a bowl of food. It smells good, but I would eat a wolf's foot I am so hungry. He places it down roughly on the table, with a wood cup and a jug of milk. I am so happy he did not bring beer. Water would have been nice, but Mother says I need milk.

The food is plain, just vegetables and mushrooms with a lump of dry bread, but it is hot and good. I am hungry, but I eat it slowly, chewing it. When I have finished the food, I drain my milk cup. I sit on the stool for a while, gazing at the fire.

Soon, pictures start to appear. I see myself in a cave. There is a huge beast, much bigger than the horse. It has wings that seem to be made of leather. They make a noise as it flaps them. Four legs have feet with claws, like an eagle, except each talon is half my length. And it has teeth. Huge teeth. I stand before it. I seem to be fearless. The beast opens its mouth and fire comes out! I hold up my staff and the fire goes round me. I blink and come back to the inn.

It is a strong vision. I do not know what it means. Suddenly, I am very tired.

I stand and take the bowl, cup and jug to the table near the landlord. He notices and nods. I think I even see a small smile. Travellers can be a rough bunch and he is like not used to one of them being helpful. Then I collect my bag and staff. As I pass him again, he says, 'Upstairs. Room at the end.'

I find the stairs and head up. My legs are so tired. There is a short passage. There is one room on the right, one on the left and one at the end. I open the door of the end room. It is very small, with a tiny window. There is a straw bed on the floor. It smells bad. I ignore it, drop my things and fall on the bed. For a moment, I look up at the ceiling and where it slopes down towards the window. I wonder about the vision beast in the cave. I have a tired moment to remember that my father's village is less than a day away, then I am asleep.

I wake to a noise. It is boots on the passage outside, heading away. Then the creak of the stairs as someone heavy descends. I have slept well and feel rested. I stretch and spend a moment wondering what the day will bring. Then I rise.

Outside, there is a barrel of water. I splash some on my face and then set off.

It is chilly, but sunny. I walk briskly and soon warm up and start to enjoy the day. There are hills to the left and right and behind me, but the way ahead is flat and I can see quite a long way. I thought the land was green, but it is not, it is greens. There are so many different greens, from the bright, sunlit-green of the grass to the shadowy, near-black of the hillside forests. Beneath my feet, the grass is worn with years of feet and carts, but tiny flowers still grow, adding colour to my path. This is a beautiful world. I remember that it will not always be so, but I also remember that what we do now, here, in this life, will affect our future. Some men get angry about things they cannot change, even things like the weather. Not many realise that they can change the world out there if they change the world inside. Now I know that, my world is getting better.

I have more fire inside because of the good sleep I had, and because of the sun, so I walk a little faster. The daylight is here, but behind me there are hills, so the sun is not quite up yet. I am not hungry, because the innkeeper gave me some bread, milk and cheese to break my fast. There was not much, but I saved half of the food for my journey. I look ahead. There is a hill I must climb. As I see it, the sun hits it and, where the lower slopes are in shadow, the top is bright green. I think my father's village must be just over that hill.

That keeps me going. Even if I was hungry, I would not want to stop now. I glance down. My arms, hands, legs and feet are very dirty with the mud and dust of the road. I have not bathed in some time, because I have not seen water. My new tunic now looks like my old one.

It is a hard climb, as the hills get steeper towards the west, but eventually I reach the top. I see a sight which I have never imagined.

I look down on a wide plain. Tiny villages are dotted here and there. Some are so small that I can barely make out the houses, but I can see columns of smoke. From the hills to the right, a growing river winds down through the green, green land. Cows sit on the grass below, and white dots of sheep are on the hill near the high stream. It is lovely, but these sights are not surprising. What is surprising is what lies ahead.

At the far end of the plain, where my path takes me, I see water. More water than I have ever seen in my short life. It is blue and dark. Can this be the sea the travellers speak of? It is endless. Well, maybe not, but it goes to the end of the world. It is the biggest single thing I have ever seen. I want to run. I want to keep running into that endless water and wash myself and float in it and drink my fill. I could never drink the millpond, so ten tens of me could never drink the sea.

I am not sure, but I think I see a village near the land's end. It looks like smoke but, if it is, it is lost in the grey of the sea. The sea! I am seeing the sea! I want to tell everyone in the village. I wish my mother was still with us. I would take some back for her to touch. But I will take some for John the miller. Perhaps he can add it to his bread for luck.

I stand for some time. The sun is at my back and I see my long shadow ahead. Eventually, I move. It is downhill all the way, now. This final part of the way is easy, but I do not fool myself. I am sure there are challenges ahead, because we always have challenges in life. How else can we grow? I feel I have grown already on this journey. Perhaps not my body, but inside I feel bigger.

Lower down, I stop and enjoy a scrap of cheese and bread. I am thirsty and look across at the stream, becoming a small river now, but I do not want to go off the way too far. I will meet the river up ahead and I can drink. The thought of the end of my journey being in sight pushes me forward.

The way is less dusty and more muddy as I descend. The plain is easy walking, though, and I make good progress. I pass through tiny villages and even manage to find a village well to take a drink. I make sure to ask someone local if I may, first.

As I pass through one place, a tall man with a dark beard comes out of his tiny home with a big stick.

'What you want here, boy?' he bellows. His voice is like thunder, yet underneath I can hear him crying. There is a small up-down sound in his voice. I make sure to be as polite as possible to someone so frightened.

'Bless you, Master, I meant no disrespect walking through your village. I am heading for the next one, with your permission,

Master.'

His angry, sad face softens, although I do not think he intended it to. After all, presenting a stern face to the world protects people. It also keeps other people away from their inside world, so they are sad. I think my soft voice, and sending out kind thoughts on the mist, have made him not fear me. He pretends to be grumpy, but nods.

'Huh. Well, then. See you don't get up to mischief, now. Huh. On your way then, lad.'

'Thank you, Master.' And I hurry off. As I go, I find myself thinking about his strange way of saying words. Why do people speak in different ways?

I am approaching my father's village. I check the map again. It is true. I am nearly there. The map shows the forest on the right, a small bend in the road, the village and, just beyond it, a hill. I am nearly at the bend.

I stop. This is it. I am about to meet my father. I am suddenly frightened, but I know not what of. Perhaps I want him to be proud, or at least not ashamed. But I am not a man. I am not even a very strong boy. I am a strange thing: a gentle boy. Can a man be proud of a gentle boy for a son? And I am dirty with the road. I would at least like to clean my face before I see him.

I turn the bend and spot a small house. A few paces farther, there is another one. And another. Smoke rises from one or two of the houses. They are all small and roughly built. I enter the centre of the village. Two people, a man and a woman, come out of the house on my left. Another woman with a small child hiding behind her skirts comes out of one on the right. Then a big man comes around the house ahead. They all head towards me. I stand still. I hold my staff upright and adjust my bag on my shoulder. They come close to me.

The big man speaks, but I do not understand his words. They are strange, but there is music in them, the same music as the man in the last village and the man with the cart. I stare at him, wide-eyed. He repeats what he said, louder. I start to shake, for I am a stranger in their village and he is getting angry. His anger spreads to the other villagers. The woman with the child repeats the man's words, none too gentle. I have to tell them I do not know their words.

'May it please you, Master, I do not know your words. I fear I am simple, Master.' Humility is a good way to put out the fires of anger.

He looks at me. Then he throws his head back and laughs. It is a musical sound, just as I heard music in his words. He mutters something to the other man, who also laughs. He looks at me and smiles, but I am not sure if the smile is friendly.

'So,' he says, 'you have travelled far, lad. What do you want here?'

Now I know his words, but the sound is strange.

'Please you, Master, I wish to see Hywel.'

He looks shocked. The others look at each other, then at him.

'Do you, now. And what would you be wanting with Hywel on such a day?'

I do not know what the day has to do with it, and I do not want to tell him, so I try to think of something true, which is not the truth.

'Please, Master. I have travelled far indeed. I have a message for Hywel. It is important. I come from Mother.'

'Mother, is it?' The look they give each other is different. It is softer, yet has a serious feel, as if they respect Mother. I doubt if they have ever met her, but perhaps Hywel has told tales.

The big man mutters to the other in the strange tongue.

'You can go up, lad. But nobody sees Hywel.' The others smile to each other.

'Bless you, Master. Where is "up"?'

He waves an arm to clear the other villagers out of the way.

'Follow the path through the houses. At the end of the village, continue up hill. When the trees thin, you will find Hywel's home. It is not far. You're welcome to visit, but nobody sees him.'

I bless and thank them. I take a few steps, then stop and turn.

'May it please you, Master, but is there water? I am so thirsty.'

'Aye, lad. The well is behind this house here.' He points to the left.

I smile and nod.

I find the well and draw up the bucket. I take the deep spoon and drink. Then I take more and pour it on my arms. I rub away the dirt. I do this again with my legs and feet. Finally, I cup my hands and throw water on my face. I rub, then throw more on, even on my ears. I cannot see my face, but when I feel it is clean, I drink some more and head off.

There are not many houses and I soon reach the end of the village. I see the small, wooded hill ahead and find the path. It twists and turns through the trees as it rises. The wood is not thick, but halfway up I look back and cannot see the village. I keep climbing.

After a short time, the land starts to flatten, the trees thin out, there is more light and I see it: my father's house. It is two buildings. The one on the left seems to be the home. The other one is rougher, perhaps used to store things.

I realise I do not know my father's trade, so I do not know what he would store. Mother said he is a wise man, so perhaps he stores plants, like her. I go up to the bigger building.

There is a door. I take a breath. I knock. Nothing.

I knock again. Nothing.

I knock a third time, a little louder, although I am suddenly timid again.

Nobody comes.

Dare I open the door? I dare not. Perhaps he is in the other building, so I walk over. There does not seem to be a door. I walk all round it, but cannot find one. This is strange.

The wind is a little stronger up here. I walk past the house a short way, as I think he is maybe looking towards the sea. I see the sea and am filled with wonder once again. But my father is not there.

I go back to the door and knock again. Nobody comes, so I sit and think.

Then, I have an idea. I stand in front of the door and close my eyes. I draw in the mist light and, as I breathe out, I send my mist into the house. It feels empty of life, until... There, in the corner, there is something. It feels like a wall to my mist. I cannot get past it, or feel into it.

Suddenly I know what I must do.

'Bless you, Master. I must see you. I hope you forgive me entering your home.'

I pause, then open the door.

It is dark inside, and there is a strange smell. Plant leaves hang from the beams. I recognise most of them, although there are a few I do not know. I step in. I try to stop my fear, not that there is like to be anything dangerous within, but I am doing a bad thing. I am going into someone's home without being invited. It is bad, but I feel this is something I must do, as if a giant, gentle hand is pushing me low in the back.

There is a table, poorly built, in the centre of the room. In the left-hand corner, a rumpled, low bed. Boots next to it. Ahead, against the far wall, stands a staff. It is fine. On it, there are signs. I cannot see them clearly, but even with the dim light from the door, I can tell it is not plain. In the far right-hand corner, there is nothing, no wall that I felt. I stop. Something is amiss. Something is strange. I feel it.

I turn on the sight. The room is full of light! It is everywhere, flashing like those stars that sometimes fall out of the sky, but which nobody ever finds. But here are so many points of light, going fast here and there. I look round. The staff is crackling with fire-red light. In the far right-hand corner, empty before, there is a ball of light. This is the wall I felt in the corner. I slowly move towards it. It shimmers, like the embers of the bone fire the next day. But this is not red and sunlight colours. It is white.

I reach out my hand. My hand wants to go in, but my mist hand stops it. It is a wall against the mist, and my mist hand is of the mist. I do not know what to do.

I will try something. I hold my hands in front of me, back to back. I put the backs of my fingers together. Then I ask the mist to extend in front of my fingertips a little. I mist wall, I reckon, might be parted by mist fingers. I concentrate. I move my hands forwards slightly, until I can feel the wall. I extend the mist a small amount. I try to use the voice of power I used on the bird.

'Open!' I command, and imagine the wall parting, like a door.

The mist parts. A gap opens. Then the mist suddenly disappears.

A man is standing in the corner.

He gazes down at me. He is very tall and powerfully built. Then he speaks. His voice is strong and gruff, but it is one I will grow to love.

'Well, now. What have we got here?'

And he smiles.

The meeting is, in some ways, unremarkable. A father and his son. A son and his long-lost and long-forgotten father. And yet, in other ways, it is extraordinary. We are, we discover, very alike. He learned the old ways from an old woman in the village. He never knew his father. His father really was lost in a war. I just believed mine was.

Over the days, he tests my knowledge. To my joy, he is impressed. He tells me that I come from a long line of wise ones. I do not consider myself wise and I tell him that. He says that is the wisest thing of all.

He is sad when I tell him about my mother, but he tells me that he already knew, because before she went into the mist, she came to say farewell. She was also a wise one, he says, but she was frightened of it. She said she felt me before I was born, and knew that I would be like my father.

As I get to know him, he asks me about my journey. I tell him all. He seems to be interested, but he stops when I tell him about the last inn and the pictures I saw in the fire. I do not know what made me tell him such a small thing, a daydream. But he says it is important. The beast I saw lives in this land. It is not real in this world, but is real in the mist land. It has a companion and they dwell under a hill, not far away. They wake when the land needs them. Sometimes, they appear in the visions and dreams of those who need them, or those who need to meet them. Father tells me I must meet one of them soon.

Father teaches me more of the old ways. He says my power must increase if good is to remain in the land. It is important that I return to my village. There is no point in having two wise ones in one area. We are spread around, all over this land. He says that sometimes we meet. He has met all of the wise ones in the land.

Recently, he says, there was a meeting, because bad men are soon to come across the sea. Many will die. All will be slaves. But the wisdom must continue. They met to decide how that could be. Some said signs, but the paper would rot over time. Another said signs on stones, but they might be destroyed by the incomers. Then one suggested pictures, as he has skills as a painter. At first, the others dismissed it, because they would have to be on paper and the paper would rot. But this one said he could make thick paper. He would make several copies, although it would take him years. There would be another meeting, so that he could explain the pictures. If the incomers found the cards, they would be told that they were merely a game. It was agreed that he should begin work. Then, a woman like Mother said that they should make signs in the mist world. If they all worked on the signs together, they would become permanent in the mist. Future wise ones would be able to see the signs and take the knowledge from them. So it was agreed. There would be a record of the old ways in this world, in the form of pictures, and in the mist world, in the form of signs with knowledge of the ways stored in them.

As I learn and practise more, I grow to love my father. He is kind and wise. And he knows what it is to be a gentle boy in a hard world. He smiles when he sees me. I feel his love too.

I stay with him for three moons and learn so much. There are bigger ways of working with the mist than those Mother taught me. He tells me the secret words and movements and how I can work with the power of plants and stones. I learn how to remove a glamour and to help people by sending back the bad thoughts and feels of others. He is impressed with my learning.

One day, when we both rise with the sun, he says it is time for my final task.

He leads me over the hill, towards the sea. Down we go, following a narrow path. There are steep drops, but I follow in my father's footsteps and feel safe. We reach the rocks. I stand on one and marvel at the sea. It is indeed vast. The little ripples I see on the millpond are caused, my father says, by the wind, are huge here and crash onto the rocks with the most beautiful noise. I told Father I wanted to drink from the sea, but he says it is not water for drinking. It will make me sick. I think that is sad. There is so much water. Nobody would go thirsty. I stare and wonder what happens at the end of the sea. I could look at it forever, but Father says we must go.

We follow the way around some rocks. There is a hole in the land. Father calls it a cave. He sits. He says he will see me when I return. Then he tells me to turn on my sight and enter the cave.

Inside, there is little light, but the sight helps me find my way. It goes deep into the cliff. I am not really afraid. After all, my father is just outside. And the mist is now my friend.

A little farther in, the top of the cave gets higher and I enter a huge chamber. In the centre, there is a small pool. Lights flash off some kind of rock in the wall. I find a piece and touch it. It is hard, like rock, but light passes through it. It makes my fingers feel strange.

I stand still. All is quiet. There is a very gentle sound from the big ripples of the sea. It is calming. Then I see something.

There are ripples on the pool. I quickly turn off my sight for a moment and the ripples are gone. I turn it on and they reappear. These are mist ripples. I wait. They grow bigger. Slowly, slowly, a claw appears. Then a huge scaled paw. I step back.

The giant beast rises out of the pool. I stand with my back against the wall. I am terrified, yet I dare not look away.

When it full out on land, it stretches its wings, opens and closes its mouth and then stands.

Then it turns and looks directly at me!

My legs turn to soup. I look into its eyes, although I think I should not. It opens its mouth. Deep in its throat, I see a light. It is like the sun and red. And growing.

It is fire! The thing takes a breath and breaths out fire!

Without thinking, I place a mist mirror in front of me. The fire shoots off to the left and right, yet I feel its force.

When it stops, I run. I go deeper into the cave. Behind me, I hear the scraping of talons. I hear the leathery flap of wings. It is following me.

I stop. I turn and face it. It stops. It looks at me. If I did not know better, it looks puzzled. Perhaps I do not know better. Perhaps I really am simple not to run away from such a fearsome beast.

It is breathing in again. More fire is coming!

Then, time seems to stop. The beast stops at a half breath.

And I remember the clearing. I remember Mother. And I remember her words.

'What is inside, appears outside, lad.'

This thing? Is it part of me? What part of me is like this? I do not breathe fire.

'Things appear out there in their own way, lad. The thing is not the same as in the mist land, but the essence is.'

Then I think of my father. He is the most powerful person I know. Yet he is gentle, like me. He is not afraid. Why am I afraid, here, now, in this cave with something of the mist?

I know I must not be afraid of it.

Time continues. The beast finishes taking its breath.

I look at it carefully. It has hard skin. It has huge teeth.

It is beautiful.

I reach out and touch it on the nose. It is not real like the rock, but it is such strong mist it feels almost real. It crackles to my touch like sparks from the bone fire.

I move over and sit next to its paw. I stroke the mighty claw.

Its huge head slowly turns towards me. Its nose comes up to mine.

Gently, so gently, it licks my chin. I stand, smile and hug it. It is not easy and I only reach a little way round its neck.

I quickly turn round. I do not know why. Perhaps to see if the cave goes deeper. When I turn back, it is gone.

Outside, Father is gone, too. I climb up the cliff to the house. He is not there. I reach out with my mist. He is not there. I collect my bag and staff from the house and go down to the village. They have not seen him.

Then I understand. I must leave. I do not need to say farewell, because he will always be with me now. And he has taught me to mist travel, so I can come if I need him. Or if the village needs him. Perhaps I can teach Mother to mist travel. I laugh out loud at this. Me! Teaching Mother something!

Now, I must go back to the village.

Back home.

Chapter 9

The journey home is just as quick as the one to Father's village. Only one thing of note happens.

I stay for a night at the wheat sheaf. I am in the same little room. That night, I have a dream.

I dream I am the man in the bed in the far future time. But he is not in bed anymore. He is at his work. It is strange work, for he does not work in a mill, nor dig the land, nor make bread, nor cheese. He does not seem to make anything. He sits in a room. In front of him is a table. On it is a small box with small signs on it. He taps things on the lower part of the box and new signs appear on the upper half. It is a wonder. I know not what the signs mean. I think they might be like the signs the priest wrote. He stops tapping sometimes and drinks from a tall, white cup. Steam rises from it. There are other people, too. They sit in silence at their tables, tapping.

When I wake, I am very sad.

The journey passes like a dream. As with the journey to my father's house, I am shown kindness by strangers. I even get a ride on a horse. I do not enjoy it any more than last time.

As I walk the final part of the path, I catch sight of the village ahead. I see the forest. In there, lies the clearing. I am excited that I am going to see Mother again. Excited, too, that I will see the village folk. I hope they are well and prosper. I should not be excited, perhaps, but I am still a boy and boys get excited.

I enter the village. It is cold here now, but not as cold as by the sea. I cannot wait to tell people about the sea. I go to the well. Nobody is around. I drink the cool, familiar water. I wonder where everyone is.

Then, I remember. It is midwinter already! The darkest day. They will be at the fire, with torches to light up the darkness. This is my task now. I must light up the darkness of people and of the world. It is a heavy task, but I am up to it. I have light inside me. And with the light comes love. Life is not easy, but I can face that too. Life is much easier when you love and are kind.

I head to the field. I smile as I pass my stone ring. I will go back there later.

Everyone is there. I see John the miller first. When he sees me, he laughs. He rushes over and grasps me by the shoulders.

'You've grown, lad. I beg pardon, young Master.' He looks ashamed for a moment. I prefer it when he is happy, so I laugh. He laughs too. Mary is there. She is with another boy. I think it is Michael, but I cannot see. I knew Mary was not for me, so I am not sad. There is nobody for me, but now I do not mind. My life is not going the way of a wife and children and I will not be a miller.

Master Thomas comes over. He looks old and tired. He tells me he is happy to see me.

'Changes are afoot, young Master. We need you now.' I nod. I tell him we will talk later.

It is wonderful to see everyone. But there is another I must see.

There is still a little daylight left, so I cut across the field and into the forest. When I get to the clearing, I go straight to the house.

It is cold. Not just because there is no fire. It is cold because there is no Mother. I know she is not in the village and I know she is not out gathering plants.

Mother is gone.

I look round for anything which will tell me where. Then I turn on my sight and call for my tall friend. He appears and I ask him the question.

'She is deep in the forest. She has a big sacred task to perform before she returns to the mist. The clearing is yours. The house is yours. The village is yours.'

'What must I do now?' I am still asking him what I should do.

I forget that it is my decision.

'That I cannot say. But I can say that you will know.' He leaves.

I sit in the room for a while. There are signs of Mother everywhere. Soon, there will be signs of me everywhere. I light a fire and soon the house is warm.

Master Thomas appears later, carrying a torch. He seems worried.

'Beg pardon, young Master. There are strange signs about and I am concerned. I met two other village heads in Dol last week. They say there are more.'

'Thank you, Thomas.' I have forgotten myself in not calling him Master Thomas. But, in a way, I think it good that I have forgotten myself. 'I will visit you first thing tomorrow.'

He thanks me and even bows a little. He moves off, then stops and turns.

He smiles. 'We are glad you are back.' He pauses. Then adds, 'Young...Father.'

I smile too.

Now I know that the lowliest of us, even a poor boy who wears rags and owns nothing, who has no friends and cannot read, yes, even a gentle boy can change the world. Each of us can choose good thoughts and kind feels. And, when we do, the world gets a little better.

I do not fear for the future. We come and go and come and go. And each time, we get a little better. A little kinder. A little more loving. And I know that in the far, far future time, when all the horrors and madness of the middle times are done, this world will be full of light. Yet each of us here, now, in our own grove of dreams can choose our way, the way which makes us happy. We can each bring a little light into the world.

Chapter 10

The next morning, the sun wakes with me.

I have a lot to do.

The mist is calling to me.

I feel it.

Things need to change.

Roundfire
FICTION

Put simply, we publish great stories. Whether it's literary or
popular, a gentle tale or a pulsating thriller, the connecting
theme in all Roundfire fiction titles is that once you pick them
up you won't want to put them down.
If you have enjoyed this book, why not tell other readers by
posting a review on your preferred book site.
Recent bestsellers from Roundfire are:

Birds of the Nile
An Egyptian Adventure
N.E. David
Ex-diplomat Michael Blake wanted a quiet birding trip up the
Nile – he wasn't expecting a revolution.
Paperback: 978-1-78279-158-4 ebook: 978-1-78279-157-7

Blood Profit$
The Lithium Conspiracy
J. Victor Tomaszek, James N. Patrick, Sr.
The blood of the many for the profits of the few... *Blood Profit$*
will take you into the cigar-smoke-filled room where American
policy and laws are really made.
Paperback: 978-1-78279-483-7 ebook: 978-1-78279-277-2

The Burden
A Family Saga
N.E. David
Frank will do anything to keep his mother and father apart. But he's carrying baggage – and it might just weigh him down ...
Paperback: 978-1-78279-936-8 ebook: 978-1-78279-937-5

The Cause
Roderick Vincent
The second American Revolution will be a fire lit from an internal spark.
Paperback: 978-1-78279-763-0 ebook: 978-1-78279-762-3

Don't Drink and Fly
The Story of Bernice O'Hanlon: Part One
Cathie Devitt
Bernice is a witch living in Glasgow. She loses her way in her life and wanders off the beaten track looking for the garden of enlightenment.
Paperback: 978-1-78279-016-7 ebook: 978-1-78279-015-0

Readers of ebooks can buy or view any of these bestsellers by clicking on the live link in the title. Most titles are published in paperback and as an ebook. Paperbacks are available in traditional bookshops. Both print and ebook formats are available online.
Find more titles and sign up to our readers' newsletter at http://www.johnhuntpublishing.com/fiction

Follow us on Facebook at
https://www.facebook.com/JHPfiction
and Twitter at https://twitter.com/JHPFiction